E. M. Delafield

The Provincial Lady Goes Further

Sharp Ink 2023

E. M. Delafield

The Provincial Lady Goes Further

Illustrated Edition

Sharp Ink, 2023
Contact: info@sharpinkbooks.com

ISBN: 978-80-283-3809-1

ILLUSTRATIONS

June 9th.–Life takes on entirely new aspect, owing to astonishing and unprecedented success of minute and unpretentious literary effort, published last December, and--incredibly--written by myself. Reactions of family and friends to this unforeseen state of affairs most interesting and varied.

Dear Vicky and Robin more than appreciative although not allowed to read book, and compare me variously to Shakespeare, Dickens, author of the Dr. Dolittle books, and writer referred to by Vicky as Lambs' Tails.

Mademoiselle--who has read book--only says *Ah, je m'en doutais bien*! which makes me uneasy, although cannot exactly say why.

Robert says very little indeed, but sits with copy of book for several evenings, and turns over a page quite often. Eventually he shuts it and says Yes. I ask what he thinks of it, and after a long silence he says that It is Funny--but does not look amused. Later he refers to financial situation--as well he may, since it has been exceedingly grave for some time past--and we agree that this ought to Make a Difference.

Conversation is then diverted to merits or demerits of the Dole--about which Robert feels strongly, and I try to be intelligent but do not bring it off--and difficulty of obtaining satisfactory raspberries from old and inferior canes.

June 12th.–Letter from Angela arrives, expressing rather needless astonishment at recent literary success. Also note from Aunt Gertrude, who says that she has not read my book and does not as a rule care about modern fiction, as *nothing* is left to the imagination. Personally, am of opinion that this, in Aunt Gertrude's case, is fortunate--but do not, of course, write back and say so.

Cissie Crabbe, on postcard picturing San Francisco--but bearing Norwich postmark as usual--says that a friend has lent her copy of book and she is looking forward to reading it. Most unlike dear Rose, who unhesitatingly spends seven-and-sixpence on acquiring it, in spite of free copy presented to her by myself on day of publication.

Customary communication from Bank, drawing my attention to a state of affairs which is only too well known to me already, enables me to write back in quite unwonted strain of optimism, assuring them that large cheque from publishers is hourly expected. Follow this letter up by much less confidently worded epistle to gentleman who has recently become privileged to act as my Literary Agent, enquiring when I may expect money from publishers, and how much.

Cook sends in a message to say that there has been a misfortune with the chops, and shall she make do with a tin of sardines? Am obliged to agree to this, as only alternative is eggs, which will be required for breakfast. (*Mem.*: Enquire into nature of alleged misfortune in the morning.)

(*Second, and more straightforward, Mem.*: Try not to lie awake cold with apprehension at having to make this enquiry, but remind myself that it is well known that all servants despise mistresses who are afraid of them, and therefore it is better policy to be firm.)

June 14th.–Note curious and rather disturbing tendency of everybody in the neighbourhood to suspect me of Putting Them into a Book. Our Vicar's Wife particularly eloquent about this, and assures me that she recognised every single character in previous literary effort. She adds that she has never had time to write a book herself, but has often thought that she would like to do so. Little things, she says--one here, another there--quaint sayings such as she hears every day of her life as she pops round the parish--Cranford, she adds in conclusion. I say Yes indeed, being unable to think of anything else, and we part.

Later on, our Vicar tells me that he, likewise, has never had time to write a book, but that if he did so, and put down some of his personal experiences, no one would ever believe them to be true. Truth, says our Vicar, is stranger than fiction.

Very singular speculations thus given rise to, as to nature of incredible experiences undergone by our Vicar. Can he have been involved in long-ago *crime passionnel*, or taken part in a duel in distant student days when sent to acquire German at Heidelberg? Imagination, always so far in advance of reason, or even propriety, carries me to further lengths, and obliges me to go upstairs and count laundry in order to change current of ideas.

Vicky meets me on the stairs and says with no preliminary Please can she go to school. Am unable to say either Yes or No at this short notice, and merely look at her in silence. She adds a brief statement to the effect that Robin went to school when he was her age, and then continues on her way downstairs, singing something of which the words are inaudible, and the tune unrecognisable, but which I have inward conviction that I should think entirely unsuitable.

Am much exercised regarding question of school, and feel that as convinced feminist it is my duty to take seriously into consideration argument quoted above.

June 15th.–Cheque arrives from publishers, via Literary Agent, who says that further instalment will follow in December. Wildest hopes exceeded, and I write acknowledgment to Literary Agent in terms of hysterical gratification that I am subsequently obliged to modify, as being undignified. Robert and I spend pleasant evening discussing relative merits of Rolls-Royce, electric light, and journey to the South of Spain--this last suggestion not favoured by Robert--but eventually decide to pay bills and Do Something about the Mortgage. Robert handsomely adds that I had better spend some of the money on myself, and what about a pearl necklace? I say Yes, to show that I am touched by his thoughtfulness, but do not commit myself to pearl necklace. Should like to suggest very small flat in London, but violent and inexplicable inhibition intervenes, and find myself quite unable to utter the words. Go to bed with flat still unmentioned, but register cast-iron resolution, whilst brushing my hair, to make early appointment in London for new permanent wave.

Also think over question of school for Vicky very seriously, and find myself coming to at least three definite conclusions, all diametrically opposed to one another.

June 16th.–Singular letter from entire stranger enquires whether I am aware that the doors of every decent home will henceforward be shut to me? Publications such as mine, he says, are harmful to art and morality alike. Should like to have this elucidated further, but signature illegible, and address highly improbable, so nothing can be done. Have recourse to waste-paper basket in absence of fires, but afterwards feel that servants or children may decipher fragments, so remove them again and ignite small private bonfire, with great difficulty, on garden path.

(*N.B.* Marked difference between real life and fiction again exemplified here. Quite massive documents, in books, invariably catch fire on slightest provocation, and are instantly reduced to ashes.)

Question of school for Vicky recrudesces with immense violence, and Mademoiselle weeps on the sofa and says that she will neither eat nor drink until this is decided. I say that I think this resolution unreasonable, and suggest Horlick's Malted Milk, to which Mademoiselle replies *Ah, ça, jamais*! and we get no further. Vicky remains unmoved throughout, and spends much time with Cook and Helen Wills. I appeal to Robert, who eventually--after long silence--says, Do as I think best.

Write and put case before Rose, as being Vicky's godmother and person of impartial views. Extreme tension meanwhile prevails in the house, and Mademoiselle continues to refuse food. Cook says darkly that it's well known as foreigners have no powers of resistance, and go to pieces-like all in a moment. Mademoiselle does not, however, go to pieces, but instead writes phenomenal number of letters, all in purple ink, which runs all over the paper whenever she cries.

I walk to the village for no other purpose than to get out of the house, which now appears to me intolerable, and am asked at the Post Office if it's really true that Miss Vicky is to be sent away, she seems such a baby. Make evasive and unhappy reply, and buy stamps. Take the longest way home, and meet three people, one of whom asks compassionately how the foreign lady is. Both the other two content themselves with being sorry to hear that we're losing Miss Vicky.

VICKY IN THE HALL.

Crawl indoors, enveloped in guilt, and am severely startled by seeing Vicky, whom I have been thinking of as a moribund exile, looking blooming, lying flat on her back in the hall eating peppermints. She says in a detached way that she needs a new sponge, and we separate without further conversation.

June 17th.–Mademoiselle shows signs of recovery, and drinks cup of tea at eleven o'clock, but relapses again later, and has une crise de nerfs. I suggest bed, and escort her there. Just as I think she can safely be left, swathed in little shawls and eiderdown quilt, she recalls me and enquires feebly if I think her health would stand life in a convent? Refuse--though I hope kindly--to discuss the question, and leave the room.

Second post brings letter from secretary of Literary Club, met once in London, informing me that I am now a member, and thoughtfully enclosing Banker's Order in order to facilitate payment of subscription, also information concerning International Congress to be held shortly in Brussels, and which she feels certain that I shall wish to attend. Decide that I *would* like to attend it, but am in some doubt as to whether Robert can be persuaded that my presence is essential to welfare of Literature. Should like to embark on immediate discussion, but all is overshadowed at lunch by devastating announcement that the Ram is not Working, and there is no water in the house. Lunch immediately assumes character of a passover, and Robert refuses cheese and departs with the gardener in order to bring Ram back to its duty--which they accomplish in about two and a half hours.

June 18th.–Dear Rose, always so definite, writes advocating school for Vicky. Co-educational, she says firmly, and Dalcroze Eurythmics. Robert, on being told this, says violently that no child of his shall be brought up amongst natives of any description. Am quite unable either to move him from this attitude, or to make him see that it is irrelevant to educational scheme at present under discussion.

Rose sends addresses of two schools, declares that she knows all about both, and invites me to go and stay with her in London and inspect them. I explain to Robert that this can be combined with new permanent wave, but Robert evidently not in a receptive mood, and remains immersed in *The Times*.

Post also brings officious communication from old Mrs. Blenkinsopp's Cousin Maud, saying that if I'm looking for a school for my brat, she could put in a word at dear old Roedean. Shall take no notice of this whatever.

June 20th.–Take bold step of writing to secretary of Literary Society to say that I will accompany its members to Brussels, and assist at Conference. Am so well aware that I shall regret this letter within an hour of writing it, that I send Vicky to village with instructions to post it instead of leaving it in box in hall as usual.

(*Query:* Does this denote extreme strength of mind or the reverse? *Answer* immediately presents itself, but see no reason for committing it to paper.)

Mademoiselle reappears in family circle, and has apparently decided that half-mourning is suitable to present crisis, as she wears black dress from which original green accessories have been removed, and fragments of mauve tulle wound round head and neck. Robert, meeting her on stairs, says kindly Mew, maln'zelle? which Mademoiselle receives with very long and involved reply, to which Robert merely returns Oh wee, and leaves her. Mademoiselle, later, tells Vicky, who repeats it to me, that it is not always education, nor even intelligence, that makes a gentleman.

Go through the linen in the afternoon, and find entirely unaccountable deficit of face-towels, but table-napkins, on the other hand, as numerous as they ever were. Blankets, as usual, require washing, but cannot be spared for the purpose, and new sheets are urgently required. Add this item to rapidly lengthening list for London. Just as I am going downstairs again, heavily speckled with fluff off blankets and reeking of camphor, enormous motor-car draws up in perfect silence at open front-door, and completely unknown woman--wearing bran-new hat about the size of a saucer with little plume over one eye--descends from it. I go forward with graceful cordiality and say, Come in, come in, which she does, and we sit and look at one another in drawing-room for ten minutes, and talk about wireless, the neighbourhood--which she evidently doesn't know--the situation in Germany, and old furniture. She turns out to be Mrs. Callington-Clay, recently come to live in house at least twenty miles away.

(Cannot imagine what can ever have induced me to call upon her, but can distinctly remember doing so, and immense relief at finding her out when I did.)

An old friend of mine, says Mrs. Callington Clay, is a neighbour of hers. Do I remember Pamela Pringle? Am obliged to say that I do not. Then perhaps I knew her as Pamela Templer-Tate? I say No again, and repress inclination to add rather tartly that I have never heard of her in my life. Mrs. C.-C. is undefeated and brazenly suggests Pamela Stevenson--whom I once more repudiate. Then, Mrs. C.-C. declares, I *must* recollect Pamela Warburton. Am by this time dazed, but admit that I did once, about twenty-three years ago, meet extraordinarily pretty girl called Pamela Warburton, at a picnic on the river. Very well then, says Mrs. C.-C., there I am! Pamela Warburton married man called Stevenson, ran away from him with man called Templer-Tate, but this, says Mrs. C.-C., a failure, and divorce ensued. She is now married to Pringle--very rich. Something in the City--Templer-Tate children live with them, but *not* Stevenson child. Beautiful old place near Somersetshire border, and Mrs. C.-C. hopes that I will call. Am still too much stunned at extraordinary activity of my contemporary to do more than say Yes, I will, and express feeble and quite insincere hope that she is as pretty as she used to be at eighteen--which is a manifest absurdity.

Finally, Mrs. C.-C. says that she enjoyed my book, and I say that that was very kind, and she asks if it takes long to write a book, and I reply Oh no, and then think it sounds conceited and wish that I had said Oh yes instead, and she departs.

Look at myself in the glass, and indulge in painful, and quite involuntary, exercise of the imagination, in which I rehearse probable description of myself that Mrs. C.-C. will give her husband on her return home. Emerge from this flight of fancy in wholly devitalised condition. Should be sorry indeed to connect this in any way with singular career of Pamela Pringle, as outlined this afternoon. At the same time, cannot deny that our paths in life have evidently diverged widely since distant occasion of river-picnic. Can conceive of no circumstances in which I should part from two husbands in succession, but am curiously depressed at unescapable conviction that my opportunities for doing so have been practically non-existent.

Write to Rose, and say that I will come and stay with her next week and inspect possible schools for Vicky, but cannot promise to patronise any of them.

June 21st.–Post agreeably diversified by most unusual preponderance of receipts over bills.

I pack for London, and explain to Robert that I am going on to Brussels for Literary Conference of international importance. He does not seem to take it in, and I explain all over again. Am sorry to realise that explanation gradually degenerates into something resembling rather a whining apology than a straightforward statement of rational intentions.

Mademoiselle appears soon after breakfast and says, coldly and elaborately, that she would Like to Speak to me when I can spare ten minutes. I say that I can spare them at once, but she replies No, no, it is not her intention to *déranger la matinée*, and she would prefer to wait, and in consequence I spend extremely unpleasant morning anticipating interview, and am quite unable to give my mind to anything at all.

(*Mem.*: This attitude positively childish, but cannot rid myself of overwhelming sensation of guilt.)

Interview with Mademoiselle takes place after lunch, and is fully as unpleasant as I anticipated.

(*Mem.*: Generalisation, so frequently heard, to the effect that things are never as bad as one expects them to be, once more proved untrue up to the hilt.)

Main conclusions to emerge from this highly distressing conference are: (a) That Mademoiselle is *pas du tout susceptible, tout au contraire*; (b) that she is profoundly *blessée*, and *froissée*, and *agacée*, and (c) that she could endure every humiliation and privation heaped upon her, if at least her supper might be brought up punctually.

This sudden introduction of entirely new element in the whole situation overcomes me completely, and we both weep.

I say, between sobs, that we both wish nothing except what is best for Vicky, and Mademoiselle replies with an offer to cut herself into a thousand pieces, and we agree to postpone further discussion for the moment.

The French not only extraordinarily exhausting to themselves and others in times of stress, but also possess very marked talent for transferring their own capacity for emotion to those with whom they are dealing.

Interesting speculation rises in my mind as to Robert's probable reactions to recent conversation with Mademoiselle, had he been present at it, but am too much exhausted to pursue subject further.

June 23rd.–Find myself in London with greatest possible relief. Rose takes one look at me, and then enquires if we have had a death in the house. I explain atmospheric conditions recently prevailing there, and she assures me that she quite understands, and the sooner I get my new permanent wave the better. Following this advice, I make early appointment.

We go to see Charles Laughton in *Payment Deferred*, and am confirmed in previous opinion that he is the most intelligent actor I have ever seen in my life. Rose says, On the *English* stage, in a cosmopolitan manner, and I say Yes, yes, very thoughtfully, and hope she does not realise that my acquaintance with any other stage is confined to performance of *La Grande Duchesse* at Boulogne, witnessed in childhood, and one sight of the Guitrys in Paris, about eleven years ago.

June 24th.–Rose takes me to visit school, which she says she is pretty certain I shall not like. Then why, I ask, go there? She replies that it is better to leave no stone unturned, and anyhow it will give me some idea of the kind of thing.

(On thinking over this reply, it seems wholly inadequate, but at the time am taken in by it.)

We go by train to large and airy red-brick establishment standing on a hill and surrounded by yellow-ochre gravel which I do not like. The Principal--colouring runs to puce and canary, and cannot avoid drawing inward parallel between her and the house--receives us in large and icy drawing-room, and is bright. I catch Rose's eye and perceive that she is unfavourably impressed, as I am myself, and that we both know that This will Never Do--nevertheless we are obliged to waste entire morning inspecting class-rooms--very light and cold--dormitories--hideously tidy, and red blankets like an institution--and gymnasium with dangerous-looking apparatus.

Children all look healthy, except one with a bandage on leg, which Principal dismisses lightly, when I enquire, as boils--and adds that child was born in India. (This event must have taken place at least ten years ago, and cannot possibly have any bearing on the case.)

Rose, behind Principal's back, forms long sentence silently with her lips, of which I do not understand one word, and then shakes her head violently. I shake mine in reply, and we are shown Chapel--chilly and unpleasant building--and Sick-room, where forlorn-looking child with inadequate little red cardigan on over school uniform is sitting in a depressed way over deadly-looking jigsaw puzzle of extreme antiquity.

The Principal says Hallo, darling, unconvincingly, and darling replies with a petrified stare, and we go out again.

I say Poor little thing! and Principal replies, more brightly than ever, that Our children love the sick-room, they have such a good time there. (This obviously untrue--and if not, reflects extremely poorly on degree of enjoyment prevalent out of the sick-room.)

Principal, who has referred to Vicky throughout as "your daughter" in highly impersonal manner, now presses on us terrific collection of documents, which she calls All Particulars, I say that I Will Write, and we return to station.

I tell Rose that really, if that is her idea of the kind of place I want--but she is apologetic, and says the next one will be quite different, and she *does*, really, know exactly what I want. I accept this statement, and we entertain ourselves on journey back to London by telling one another how much we disliked the Principal, her establishment, and everything connected with it.

I even go so far as to suggest writing to parents of bandaged child with boils, but as I do not know either her name or theirs, this goes no further.

(Am occasionally made uneasy at recollection of pious axiom dating back to early childhood, to the effect that every idle word spoken will one day have to be accounted for. If this is indeed fact, can foresee a thoroughly well-filled Eternity for a good many of us.)

June 25th.–Undergo permanent wave, with customary interludes of feeling that nothing on earth can be worth it, and eventual conviction that it *was*.

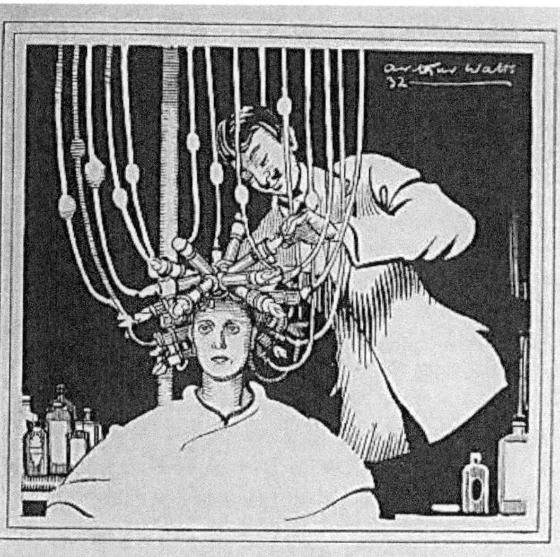

UNDERGO PERMANENT WAVE

The hairdresser tells me that he has done five heads this week, all of which came up beautifully. He also assures me that I shall *not* be left alone whilst the heating is on, and adds gravely that no client ever is left alone at that stage--which has a sinister sound, and terrifies me. However, I emerge safely, and my head is also declared to have come up beautifully--which it has.

I go back to Rose's flat, and display waves, and am told that I look fifteen years younger--which leaves me wondering what on earth I could have looked like before, and how long I have been looking it.

Rose and I go shopping, and look in every shop to see if my recent publication is in window, which it never is except once. Rose suggests that whenever we do not see book, we ought to go in and ask for it, with expressions of astonishment, and I agree that certainly we ought. We leave it at that.

June 26th.–Inspect another school, and think well of Headmistress, also of delightful old house and grounds. Education, however, appears to be altogether given over to Handicrafts--green raffia mats and mauve paper boxes--and Self-expression--table manners of some of the pupils far from satisfactory. Decide, once more, that this does not meet requirements, and go away again.

Rose takes me to a party, and introduces me to several writers, one male and eight females. I wear new mauve frock, purchased that afternoon, and thanks to that and permanent wave, look nice, but must remember to have evening shoes re-covered, as worn gold brocade quite unsuitable.

Tall female novelist tells me that she is a friend of a friend of a friend of mine--which reminds me of popular song--and turns out to be referring to young gentleman known to me as Jahsper, once inflicted upon us by Miss Pankerton. Avoid tall female novelist with horror and dismay for the remainder of the evening.

June 28th.–Letter reaches me forwarded from home, written by contemporary of twenty-three years ago, then Pamela Warburton and now Pamela Pringle. She has heard so much of me from Mrs. Callington-Clay (who has only met me once herself and cannot possibly have anything whatever to say about me, except that I exist) and would so much like to meet me again. Do I remember picnic on the river in dear old days now so long ago? Much, writes Pamela Pringle--as well she may--has happened since then, and perhaps I have heard that after many troubles, she has at last found Peace, she trusts lasting. (Uncharitable reflection crosses my mind that P. P., judging from outline of her career given by Mrs. Callington-Clay, had better not count too much upon this, if by Peace she means matrimonial stability.)

Will I, pathetically adds Pamela, come and see her soon, for the sake of old times?

Write and reply that I will do so on my return--though less for the sake of old times than from lively curiosity, but naturally say nothing about this (extremely inferior) motive.

Go to large establishment which is having a Sale, in order to buy sheets. Find, to my horror, that I return having not only bought sheets, but blue lace tea-gown, six pads of writing-paper, ruled, small hair-slide, remnant of red brocade, and reversible black-and-white bath-mat, with slight flaw in it.

Cannot imagine how any of it happened.

Rose and I go to French film called *Le Million*, and are much amused. Coming out we meet Canadian, evidently old friend of Rose's, who asks us both to dine and go to theatre on following night, and says he will bring another man. We accept, I again congratulate myself on new and successful permanent wave.

Conscience compels me to hint to Rose that I have really come to London in order to look for schools, and she says Yes, yes, there is one more on her list that she is certain I shall like, and we will go there this afternoon.

I ask Rose for explanation of Canadian friend, and she replies that they met when she was travelling in Italy, which seems to me ridiculous. She adds further that he is very nice, and has a mother in Ontario. Am reminded of 0llendorf, but do not say so.

After lunch--cutlets excellent, and quite unlike very uninspiring dish bearing similar name which appears at frequent intervals at home--go by Green Line bus to Mickleham, near Leatherhead. Perfect school is discovered, Principal instantly enquires Vicky's name and refers to her by it afterwards, house, garden and children alike charming, no bandages to be seen anywhere, and Handicrafts evidently occupy only rational amount of attention. Favourite periodical *Time and Tide* lies on table, and Rose, at an early stage, nods at me with extreme vehemence behind Principal's back. I nod in return, but feel they will think better of me if I go away without committing myself. This I succeed in doing, and after short conversation concerning fees, which are not unreasonable, we take our departure. Rose enthusiastic, I say that I must consult Robert,–but this is mostly *pour la forme*, and we feel that Vicky's fate is decided.

June 29th.–Colossal success of evening's entertainment offered by Rose's Canadian. He brings with him delightful American friend, we dine at exotic and expensive restaurant, filled with literary and theatrical celebrities, and go to a revue. American friend says that he understands I have written a book, but does not seem to think any the worse of me for this, and later asks to be told name of book, which he writes down in a business-like way on programme, and puts into his pocket.

They take us to the Berkeley, where we remain until two o'clock in the morning, and are finally escorted to Rose's flat. Have I, asks the American, also got a flat? I say No, unfortunately I have not, and we all agree that this is a frightful state of things and should be remedied immediately. Quite earnest discussion ensues on the pavement, with taxi waiting at great expense.

At last we separate, and I tell Rose that this has been the most wonderful evening I have known for years, and she says that champagne often does that, and we go to our respective rooms.

Query presents itself here: Are the effects of alcohol always wholly to be regretted, or do they not sometimes serve useful purpose of promoting self-confidence? *Answer*, to-night, undoubtedly Yes, but am not prepared to make prediction as to to-morrow's reactions.

June 30th.–Realise with astonishment that Literary Conference in Brussels is practically due to begin, and that much has yet to be done with regard to packing, passport, taking of tickets and changing money. Much of this accomplished, with help of Rose, and I write long letter to Robert telling him where to telegraph in case anything happens to either of the children.

Decide to travel in grey-and-white check silk.

Ring up Secretary of Literary Club in order to find out further details, and am told by slightly reproachful subordinate that Conference started this morning, and everybody else crossed yesterday. Am stunned by this, but Rose, as usual, is bracing, and says What does it Matter, and on second thoughts, agree with her that it doesn't. We spend agreeable evening, mostly talking about ourselves, and Rose says Why go to Belgium at all? but at this I jib, and say that Plans are Plans, and anyhow, I want to see the country. We leave it at that.

July 2nd.–Cannot decide whether it is going to be hot or cold, but finally decide Hot, and put on grey-and-white check silk in which I think I look nice, with small black hat. Sky immediately clouds over and everything becomes chilly. Finish packing, weather now definitely cold, and am constrained to unpack blue coat and skirt, with Shetland jumper, and put it on in place of grey-and-white check, which I reluctantly deposit in suit-case, where it will get crushed. Black hat now becomes unsuitable, and I spend much time trying on remaining hats in wardrobe, to the total of three.

Suddenly discover that it is late--boat-train starts in an hour--and take taxi to station. Frightful conviction that I shall miss it causes me to sit on extreme edge of seat in taxi, leaning well forward, in extraordinarily uncomfortable position that subsequently leads to acute muscular discomfort. However, either this, or other cause unspecified, leads to Victoria being reached with rather more than twenty minutes to spare.

A porter finds me a seat, and I ask if there will be food on the train. He disquietingly replies: Food, *if at all*, will be on the boat. Decide to get some fruit, and find my way to immense glass emporium, where I am confronted by English Peaches, One shilling apiece, Strawberries in baskets, and inferior peaches, of unspecified nationality, at tenpence. Am horrified, in the midst of all this, to hear myself asking for two bananas in a bag, please. Should not be in the least surprised if the man refused to supply them. He does not, however, do so, and I return to the train, bananas and all.

Embarkation safely accomplished. Crossing more successful than usual, and only once have recourse to old remedy of reciting *An Austrian army awfully arrayed.*

LITERARY CLUB MEMBERS

Reach Brussels, and am at Hotel Britannia by eight o'clock. All is red plush, irrelevant gilt mouldings, and Literary Club members. I look at them, and they at me, with horror and distrust. (*Query:* Is not this reaction peculiar to the English, and does patriotism forbid conviction that it is by no means to be admired? Americans totally different, and, am inclined to think, much nicer in consequence.)

Find myself at last face to face with dear old friend, Emma Hay, author of many successful plays. Dear old friend is wearing emerald green, which would be trying to almost anyone, and astonishing quantity of rings, brooches and necklaces. She says, Fancy seeing me here! and have I broken away at last? I say, No, certainly not, and suggest dinner. Am introduced by Emma to any number of literary lights, most of whom seem to be delegates from the Balkans.

(*N.B.* Should be very, very sorry if suddenly called upon to give details as to situation, and component parts, of the Balkans.)

Perceive, without surprise, that the Balkans are as ignorant of my claims to distinction as I of theirs, and we exchange amiable conversation about Belgium,–King Albert popular, Queen Elizabeth shingled, and dresses well--and ask one another if we know Mr. Galsworthy, which none of us do.

July 3rd.–Literary Conference takes place in the morning. The Balkans very eloquent. They speak in French, and are translated by inferior interpreters into English. Am sorry to find attention wandering on several occasions to entirely unrelated topics, such as Companionate Marriage, absence of radiators in Church at home, and difficulty in procuring ice. Make notes on back of visiting-card, in order to try and feel presence at Conference in any way justified. Find these again later, and discover that they refer to purchase of picture-postcards for Robin and Vicky, memorandum that blue evening dress requires a stitch before it can be worn again, and necessity for finding out whereabouts of Messrs. Thos. Cook & Son, in case I run short of money--which I am almost certain to do.

Emma introduces Italian delegate, who bows and kisses my hand. Feel certain that Robert would not care for this Continental custom. Conference continues. I sit next to (moderately) celebrated poet, who pays no attention to me, or anybody else. Dear Emma, always so energetic, takes advantage of break in Conference to introduce more Balkans, both to me and to adjacent poet. The latter remains torpid throughout, and elderly Balkan, who has mistakenly endeavoured to rouse him to conversation, retires with embittered ejaculation: *Ne vous réveillez pas, monsieur.*

Close of Conference, and general conversation, Emma performing many introductions, including me and Italian delegate once more. Italian delegate remains apparently unaware that he has ever set eyes on me before, and can only conclude that appearance and personality alike have failed to make slightest impression.

Find myself wondering why I came to Belgium at all. Should like to feel that it was in the interests of literature, but am doubtful, and entirely disinclined to probe further. Feminine human nature sometimes very discouraging subject for speculation.

Afternoon devoted to sight-seeing. We visit admirable Town Hall, are received by Mayor, who makes speech, first in English, and then all over again in French, other speeches are made in return, and energetic Belgian gentleman takes us all over Brussels on foot. Find myself sympathising with small and heated delegate,–country unknown, but accent very odd--who says to me dejectedly, as we pace the cobbles: *C'est un tour de la Belgique à pied, hein*?

July 5th.–Extreme exhaustion overwhelms me, consequent on excessive sight-seeing. I ask Emma if she would think it unsporting if I evaded charabanc expedition to Malines this afternoon, and she looks pained and astonished and says Shall she be quite honest? I lack courage to say how much I should prefer her not to be honest at all, and Emma assures me that it is my duty, in the interests of literature and internationalism alike, to go to Malines. She adds that there will be tea in the Town Hall--which I know means more speeches--and that afterwards we shall hear a Carillon Concert.

Shall she, Emma adds, wear her green velvet, which will be too hot, or her Rumanian peasant costume, which is too tight, but may please our Rumanian delegates? I advocate sacrificing our Rumanian delegates without hesitation.

Large motor-bus is a great relief after so much walking, and I take my seat beside an unknown French lady with golden hair and a bust, but am beckoned away by Emma, who explains in agitation that the French lady has come to Belgium entirely in order to see something of a Polish friend, because otherwise she never gets away from her husband. Am conscious of being distinctly shocked by this, but do not say so in case Emma should think me provincial. Yield my place to the Polish friend, who seems to me to be in need of soap and water and a shave, but perhaps this mere insular prejudice, and go and sit next to an American young gentleman, who remains indifferent to my presence.

(*Query:* Does this complaisancy on my part amount to countenancing very singular relation which obviously obtains between my fellow-littérateurs? If so, have not the moral courage to do anything about it.)

Nothing of moment passes during drive, except that the French lady takes off her hat and lays her head on her neighbour's shoulder, and that I hear Belgian delegate enquiring of extremely young and pretty Englishwoman: What is the English for Autobus, to which she naïvely returns that: It is Charabanc.

Arrival at Town Hall, reception, speeches and tea take place exactly as anticipated, and we proceed in groups, and on foot, to the Carillon Concert. American neighbour deserts me--have felt certain all along that he always meant to do so at earliest possible opportunity--and I accommodate my pace to that of extremely elderly Belgian, who says that it is certainly not for us to emulate *les jeunes* on a hot day like this, and do I realise that for *nous autres* there is always danger of an apoplexy? Make no reply to this whatever, but inwardly indulge in cynical reflections about extremely poor reward afforded in this life to attempted acts of good nature.

July 6th.–Final Conference in the morning, at which much of importance is doubtless settled, but cannot follow owing to reading letters from home, which have just arrived. Robert says that he hopes I am enjoying myself, and we have had one and a quarter inches of rain since Thursday, and bill for roof-repairs has come in and is even more than he expected. Robin and Vicky write briefly, but affectionately, information in each case being mainly concerned with food, and--in Robin's case--progress of Stamp Collection, which now, he says, must be worth 10d. or 11d. altogether.

Inspection of Antwerp Harbour by motor-launch takes place in the afternoon, and the majority of us sit with our backs to the rails and look at one another. Conversation in my immediate vicinity concerns President Hoover, the novels of J. B. Priestley and *Lady Chatterley's Lover*, which everyone except myself seems to have read and admired. I ask unknown lady on my right if it can be got from the Times Book Club, and she says No, only in Paris, and advises me to go there before I return home. Cannot, however, feel that grave additional expense thus incurred would be justified, and in any case could not possibly explain *détour* satisfactorily to Robert.

Disembark from motor-launch chilled and exhausted, and with conviction that my face has turned pale-green. Inspection in pocket-mirror more than confirms this intuition. Just as I am powdering with energy, rather than success, Emma--vitality evidently unimpaired either by society of fellow-writers or by motor-launch approaches with Italian delegate, and again introduces us.

All is brought to a close by State Banquet this evening, for which everyone--rather strangely--has to pay quite a large number of francs. Incredible number of speeches delivered: ingenious system prevails by which bulb of crimson light is flashed on as soon as any speech has exceeded two and a half minutes. Unfortunately this has no effect whatever on many of our speakers, who disregard it completely. Dear Emma not amongst these, and makes admirably concise remarks which are met with much applause. I sit next to unknown Dutchman--who asks if I prefer to speak English, French, Dutch or German--and very small and dusty Oriental, who complains of the heat.

We rise at eleven o'clock, and dancing is suggested. Just as I move quietly away in search of cloak, taxi and bed, Emma appears and says This will never do, and I must come and dance. I refuse weakly, and she says Why not? to which the only rational reply would be that I have splitting headache, and am not interested in my colleagues nor they in me. Do not, needless to say, indulge in any such candour, and result is that I am thrust by Emma upon American young gentleman for a foxtrot. I say that I dance very badly, and he says that no one can ever keep step with him. Both statements turn out to be perfectly true, and I go back to Hotel dejected, and remind myself that It is Useless to struggle against Middle-age.

July 8th.–Embark for England, not without thankfulness. Am surprised to discover that I have a sore throat, undoubted result of persistent endeavour to out-screech fellow-members of Literary Club for about a week on end.

Emma travels with me, and says that she is camping in Wales all next month, and will I join her? Nothing but a tent, and she lives on bananas and milk chocolate. Associations with the last words lead me to reply absently that the children would like it, at which Emma seems hurt and enquires whether I intend to spend my life between the nursery and the kitchen? The only possible answer to this is that I like it, and discussion becomes animated and rather painful.

Emma, on board, avoids me, and I am thrown into society of insufferable male novelist, who is interested in Sex. He has an immense amount to say about it, and we sit on deck for what seems like hours and hours. He says at last that he hopes he is not boring me, and I hear myself, to my incredulous horror, saying pleasantly No, not at all--at which he naturally goes on.

EMMA IN WALES

Become gradually paralysed, and unable to think of anything in the world except how I can get away, but nothing presents itself. At last I mutter something about being cold--which I am--and he at once suggests walking round and round the deck, while he tells me about extraordinarily distressing marriage customs prevalent amongst obscure tribes of another hemisphere. Find myself wondering feebly whether, if I suddenly jumped overboard, he would stop talking. Am almost on the verge of trying this experiment when Emma surges up out of deck-chair and enveloping rugs, and says Oh there I am, she has been looking for me everywhere.

Sink down beside her with profound gratitude, and male novelist departs, assuring me that he will remember to send me list of books on return to London. Can remember nothing whatever of any books discussed between us, but am absolutely convinced that they will be quite unsuitable for inclusion in respectable book-shelves.

Emma is kind, says that she didn't mean a single word she said--(have quite forgotten by this time what she did say, but do not tell her so)–and assures me that what I need is a good night's rest. She then tells me all about a new Trilogy that she is planning to write and which ought to be published by 1938, and also about her views on Bertrand Russell, the works of Stravinsky, and Relativity. At one o'clock in the morning we seek our cabin, last thing I hear being Emma's positive assurance that I need not be afraid of America's influence on the English stage...

July 9th.–London regained, though not before I have endured further spate of conversation from several lights of literature.

(*Query:* Does not very intimate connection exist between literary ability and quite inordinate powers of talk? And if so, is it not the duty of public-spirited persons to make this clear, once for all? *Further Query:* How?)

Part from everybody with immeasurable relief, and wholly disingenuous expressions of regret.

Find Rose in great excitement, saying that she has found the Very Thing. I reply firmly If Bertrand Russell for Vicky, then *No*, to which Rose rejoins that she does not know what I am talking about, but she has found me a flat. Logical and straightforward reply to this would be that I am not looking for a flat, and cannot afford one. This, however, eludes me altogether, and I accompany Rose, via bus No. 19, to Doughty Street, where Rose informs me that Charles Dickens once lived. She adds impressively that she *thinks*, but is not sure, that Someone-or-other was born at a house in Theobald's Road, close by. Brisk discussion as to relative merits of pronouncing this as "Theobald" or "Tibbald" brings us to the door of the flat, where ground-floor tenant hands us keys. Entirely admirable first-floor flat is revealed, unfurnished, and including a bedroom, sitting-room, bathroom and kitchen. To the last, I say that I would rather go out for all my meals than do any cooking at all. Then, Rose replies with presence of mind, use it as a box-room. We make intelligent notes of questions to be referred to agents--Rose scores highest for sound common-sense enquiries as to Power being Laid On and Rates included in Rent--and find soon afterwards that I am committed to a three-year tenancy, with power to sub-let, and a choice of wall-papers, cost not to exceed two shillings a yard. From September quarter, says the agent, and suggests a deposit of say two pounds, which Rose and I muster with great difficulty, mostly in florins.

Go away feeling completely dazed, and quite unable to imagine how I shall explain any of it to Robert. This feeling recrudesces violently in the middle of the night, and in fact keeps me awake for nearly an hour, and is coupled with extremely agitating medley of quite unanswerable questions, such as What I am to Do about a Telephone, and who will look after the flat when I am not in it, and what about having the windows cleaned? After this painful interlude I go to sleep again, and eventually wake up calm, and only slightly apprehensive. This, however, may be the result of mental exhaustion.

July 11th.–Return home, and am greeted with customary accumulation of unexpected happenings, such as mysterious stain on ceiling of spare bedroom, enormous bruise received by Vicky in unspecified activity connected with gardener's bicycle, and letters which ought to have been answered days ago and were never forwarded. Am struck by the fact that tea is very nasty, with inferior bought cake bearing mauve decorations, and no jam. Realisation that I shall have to speak to cook about this in the morning shatters me completely, and by the time I go to bed, Rose, London and Doughty Street have receded into practically forgotten past.

Robert comes to bed soon after one--am perfectly aware that he has been asleep downstairs--and I begin to tell him about the flat. He says that it is very late, and that he supposes the washerwoman puts his pyjamas through the mangle, as the buttons are always broken. I brush this aside and revert to the flat, but without success. I then ask in desperation if Robert would like to hear about Vicky's school; he replies Not now, and we subside into silence.

July 12th.–Cook gives notice.

July 14th.–Pamela Warburton--now Pamela Pringle--and I meet once again, since I take the trouble to motor into the next county in response to an invitation to tea.

Enormous house, with enormous gardens--which I trust not to be asked to inspect--and am shown into room with blue ceiling and quantities of little dogs, all barking. Pamela surges up in a pair of blue satin pyjamas and an immense cigarette-holder, and astonishes me by looking extremely young and handsome. Am particularly struck by becoming effect of brilliant coral lip-stick, and insane thoughts flit through my mind of appearing in Church next Sunday similarly adorned, and watching the effect upon our Vicar. This flight of fancy routed by Pamela's greetings, and introduction to what seems like a small regiment of men, oldest and baldest of whom turns out to be Pringle. Pamela then tells them that she and I were at school together--which is entirely untrue--and that I haven't changed in the least--which I should like to believe, and can't--and offers me a cocktail, which I recklessly accept in order to show

how modern I am. Do not, however, enjoy it in the least, and cannot see that it increases my conversational powers. Am moreover thrown on my beam-ends at the very start by unknown young man who asks if I am not the Colonel's wife? Repudiate this on the spot with startled negative, and then wonder if I have not laid foundations of a scandal, and try to put it right by feeble addition to the effect that I do not even know the Colonel, and am married to somebody quite different. Unknown young man looks incredulous, and at once begins to talk about interior decoration, the Spanish Royal Family, and modern lighting. I respond faintly, and try to remember if Pamela P. always had auburn hair. Should moreover very much like to know how she has collected her men, and totally eliminated customary accompanying wives.

Later on, have an opportunity of enquiring into these phenomena, as P. P. takes me to see children. Do not like to ask much about them, for fear of becoming involved in very, very intricate questions concerning P.'s matrimonial extravagances.

Nurseries are entirely decorated in white, and furnished exactly like illustrated articles in *Good Housekeeping*, even to coloured frieze all round the walls. Express admiration, but am inwardly depressed, at contrast with extraordinarily inferior school-room at home. Hear myself agreeing quite firmly with P. P. that it is most important to Train the Eye from the very beginning--and try not to remember large screen covered with scraps from illustrated papers; extremely hideous Brussels carpet descended from dear Grandmamma, and still more hideous oil-painting of quite unidentified peasant carrying improbable-looking jar--all of which form habitual surroundings of Robin and Vicky.

P. P. calls children, and they appear, looking, if possible, even more expensive and hygienic than their nursery. Should be sorry to think that I pounce with satisfaction on the fact that all of them wear spectacles, and one a plate, but cannot quite escape suspicion that this is so. All have dark hair, perfectly straight, and am more doubtful than ever about P.'s auburn waves.

We all exchange handshakes, I say that I have a little boy and a little girl at home--which information children rightly receive with brassy indifference--Pamela shows me adjoining suite of night-nurseries, tiled bathroom and kitchen, and says how handy it is to have a nursery wing quite apart from the rest of the house, and I reply Yes indeed, as if I had always found it so, and say good-bye to the little Spectacles with relief.

Pamela, on the way downstairs, is gushing, and hopes that she is going to see a great deal of me, now that we are neighbours. Forty-one miles does not, in my opinion, constitute being neighbours, but I make appropriate response, and Pamela says that some day we must have a long, long talk. Cannot help hoping this means that she is going to tell me the story of Stevenson, Templer-Tate and Co.

(*N.B.* Singular and regrettable fact that I should not care twopence about the confidences of P. P. except for the fact that they are obviously bound to contain references to scandalous and deplorable occurrences, which would surely be better left in oblivion?)

Drive forty-one miles home again, thinking about a new cook--practically no ray of hope anywhere on horizon here--decision about Vicky's school, Mademoiselle's probable reactions to final announcement on the point, and problem in regard to furnishing of Doughty Street flat.

July 17th.–Am obliged to take high line with Robert and compel him to listen to me whilst I tell him about the flat. He eventually gives me his attention, and I pour out torrents of eloquence, which grow more and more feeble as I perceive their effect upon Robert. Finally he says, kindly but gloomily, that he does not know what can have possessed me--neither do I, by this time--but that he supposes I had to do *something*, and there is a good deal too much furniture here, so some of it can go to Doughty Street.

At this I revive, and we go into furniture in detail, and eventually discover that the only things we can possibly do without are large green glass vase from drawing-room, small maple-wood table with one leg missing, framed engraving of the Prince Consort from bathroom landing, and strip of carpet believed--without certainty--to be put away in attic. This necessitates complete readjustment of furniture question on entirely new basis. I become excited, and Robert says Well, it's my own money, after all, and Why not leave it alone for the present, and we can talk about it again later? Am obliged to conform to this last suggestion, as he follows it up by immediately leaving the room.

Write several letters to Registry Offices, and put advertisement in local *Gazette*, regarding cook. Advertisement takes much time and thought, owing to feeling that it is better to be honest and let them know the worst at once, and equally strong feeling that situation must be made to sound as attractive as possible. Finally put in "good outings" and leave out "oil lamps only" but revert to candour with "quiet country place" and "four in family".

Am struck, not for the first time, with absolutely unprecedented display of talent and industry shown by departing cook, who sends up hitherto undreamed-of triumphs of cookery, evidently determined to show us what we are losing.

July 19th.–Receive two replies to *Gazette* advertisement, one from illiterate person who hopes we do not want dinner in the night--(*Query:* Why should we?)–and another in superior, but unpleasant, handwriting demanding kitchen-maid, colossal wages and improbable concessions as to times off. Reason tells me to leave both unanswered; nevertheless find myself sending long and detailed replies and even--in case of superior scribe--suggesting interview.

Question of Vicky's school recrudesces, demanding and receiving definite decisions. Am confronted with the horrid necessity of breaking this to Mademoiselle. Decide to do so immediately after breakfast, but find myself inventing urgent errands in quite other parts of the house, which occupy me until Mademoiselle safely started for walk with Vicky.

(*Query:* Does not moral cowardice often lead to very marked degree of self-deception? *Answer:* Most undoubtedly yes.)

Decide to speak to Mademoiselle after lunch. At lunch, however, she seems depressed, and says that the weather *lui Porte sur les nerfs*, and I feel better perhaps leave it till after tea. Cannot decide if this is true consideration, or merely further cowardice. Weather gets steadily worse as day goes on, and is probably going to *porter sur les nerfs* of Mademoiselle worse than ever, but register cast-iron resolution not to let this interfere with speaking to her after Vicky has gone to bed.

Robin's Headmaster's wife writes that boys are all being sent home a week earlier, owing to case of jaundice, which is--she adds--*not* catching. Can see neither sense nor logic in this, but am delighted at having Robin home almost at once. This satisfaction, most regrettably, quite unshared by Robert. Vicky, however, makes up for it by noisy and prolonged display of enthusiasm. Mademoiselle, as usual, is touched by this, exclaims *Ah, quel bon petit coeur!* and reduces me once more to despair at thought of the blow in store for her. Find myself desperately delaying Vicky's bed-time, in prolonging game of Ludo to quite inordinate lengths.

THE SOCKS LADY

Just as good-night is being said by Vicky, I am informed that a lady is the back door, and would like to speak to me, please. The lady turns out to be in charge of battered perambulator, filled with apparently hundreds of green cardboard boxes, all--she alleges--containing garments knitted by herself. She offers to display them; I say No, thank you, not to-day, and she immediately does so. They all strike me as frightful in the extreme.

Painful monologue ensues, which includes statements about husband having been a Colonel in the Army, former visits to Court, and staff of ten indoor servants. Am entirely unable to believe any of it, but do not like to say so, or even to interrupt so much fluency. Much relieved when Robert appears, and gets rid of perambulator, boxes and all, apparently by power of the human eye alone, in something under three minutes.

(He admits, later, to having parted with half a crown at back gate, but this I think touching, and much to his credit.)

Robert, after dinner, is unwontedly talkative--about hay--and do not like to discourage him, so bed-time is reached with Mademoiselle still unaware of impending doom.

July 21st.–Interview two cooks, results wholly unfavourable. Return home in deep depression, and Mademoiselle offers to make me a tisane--but substitutes tea at my urgent request--and shows so much kindness that I once more postpone painful task of enlightening her as to immediate future.

July 22nd.–Return of Robin, who is facetious about jaundice case--supposed to be a friend of his--and looks well. He eats enormous tea and complains of starvation at school. Mademoiselle says *Le pauvre gosse!* and produces packet of Menier chocolate, which Robin accepts with gratitude--but am only too well aware that this alliance is of highly ephemeral character.

I tell Robin about Doughty Street flat and he is most interested and sympathetic, and offers to make me a box for shoes, or a hanging bookshelf, whichever I prefer. We then adjourn to garden and all play cricket, Mademoiselle's plea for *une balle de caoutchouc* being, rightly, ignored by all. Robin kindly allows me to keep wicket, as being post which I regard as least dangerous, and Vicky is left to bowl, which she does very slowly, and with many wides. Helen Wills puts in customary appearance, but abandons us on receiving cricket-ball on front paws. After what feels like several hours of this, Robert appears, and game at once takes on entirely different--and much brisker--aspect. Mademoiselle immediately says firmly *Moi, je ne joue plus* and walks indoors. Cannot feel that this is altogether a sporting spirit, but have private inner conviction that nothing but moral cowardice prevents my following her example. However, I remain at my post--analogy with Casabianca indicated here--and go so far as to stop a couple of balls and miss one or two catches, after which I am told to bat, and succeed in scoring two before Robin bowls me.

Cricket decidedly not my game, but this reflection closely followed by unavoidable enquiry: What is? Answer comes there none.

July 23rd.–Take the bull by the horns, although belatedly, and seek Mademoiselle at two o'clock in the afternoon--Vicky resting, and Robin reading *Sherlock Holmes* on front stairs, which he prefers to more orthodox sitting-rooms--May I, say I feebly, sit down for a moment?

Mademoiselle at once advances her own armchair and says *Ah, ça me fait du bien de recevoir madame dans mon petit domaine*–which makes me feel worse than ever.

Extremely painful half-hour follows. We go over ground that we have traversed many times before, and reach conclusions only to unreach them again, and the whole ends, as usual, in floods of tears and mutual professions of esteem. Emerge from it all with only two solid facts to hold on to--that Mademoiselle is to return to her native land at an early date, and that Vicky goes to school at Mickleham in September.

(*N.B.* When announcing this to Vicky, must put it to her in such a way: that she is neither indecently joyful at emancipation, nor stonily indifferent to Mademoiselle's departure. Can foresee difficult situation arising here, and say so to Robert, who tells me not to cross my bridges before I get to them--which I consider aggravating.)

Spend a great deal of time writing to Principal of Vicky's school, to dentist for appointments, and to Army and Navy Stores for groceries. Am quite unable to say why this should leave me entirely exhausted in mind and body--but it does.

July 25th.–Go to Exeter in order to interview yet another cook, and spend exactly two hours and twenty minute in Registry Office waiting for her to turn up--which she never does. At intervals, I ask offenive-looking woman in orange *béret*, who sits at desk, What she thinks can have Happened, and she replies that she couldn't say, she's sure, and such a thing has never happened in the office before, never--which makes me feel that it is all my fault.

Harassed-looking lady in transparent pink mackintosh trails in, and asks for a cook-general, but is curtly dismissed by orange *béret* with assurance that cooks-general for the country are not to be found. If they were, adds the orange *béret* cynically, her fortune would have been made long ago. The pink mackintosh, like Queen Victoria, is not amused, and goes out again. She is succeeded by a long interval, during which the orange *béret* leaves the room and returns with a cup of tea, and I look--for the fourteenth time--at only available literature, which consists of ridiculous little periodical called "Do the Dead Speak?" and disembowelled copy of the *Sphere* for February 1929.

Orange *béret* drinks tea, and has long and entirely mysterious conversation conducted in whispers with client who looks like a charwoman.

Paralysis gradually invades me, and feel that I shall never move again--but eventually, of course, do so, and find that I have very nearly missed bus home again. Evolve scheme for selling house and going to live in hotel, preferably in South of France, and thus disposing for ever of servant question. Am aware that this is not wholly practicable idea, and would almost certainly lead to very serious trouble with Robert.

(*Query:* Is not theory mistaken, which attributes idle and profitless day-dreaming to youth? Should be much more inclined to add it to many other unsuitable and unprofitable weaknesses of middle-age.)

Spend the evening with children, who are extraordinarily energetic, and seem surprised when I refuse invitation to play tip-and-run, but agree, very agreeably, to sit still instead and listen to *Vice Versa* for third time of reading.

July 26th.–Spirited discussion at breakfast concerning annual problem of a summer holiday. I hold out for Brittany, and produce little leaflet obtained from Exeter Travel Agency, recklessly promising unlimited sunshine, bathing and extreme cheapness of living. Am supported by Robin--who adds a stipulation that he is not to be asked to eat frogs. Mademoiselle groans, and says that the crossing will assuredly be fatal to us all and this year is one notable for *naufrages.* At this stage Vicky confuses the issue by urging travel by air, and further assures us that in France all the little boys have their hair cut exactly like convicts. Mademoiselle becomes *froissée,* and says *Ah non, par exemple, je ne m' offense pas, moi, mais ça tout de même*–and makes a long speech, the outcome of which is that Vicky has neither heart nor common sense, at which Vicky howls, and Robert says My God and cuts ham.

Discussion then starts again on a fresh basis, with Vicky outside the door where she can be heard shrieking at intervals--but this mechanical, rather than indicative of serious distress--and Mademoiselle showing a tendency to fold her lips tightly and repeat that nobody is to pay any attention to her wishes about anything whatever.

I begin all over again about Brittany, heavily backed by Robin, who says It is well known that all foreigners live on snails. (At this I look apprehensively at Mademoiselle, but fortunately she has not heard.)

Robert's sole contribution to discussion is that England is quite good enough for him.

(Could easily remind Robert of many occasions, connected with Labour Government activities in particular, when England has been far from good enough for him--but refrain.)

Would it not, I urge, be an excellent plan to shut up the house for a month, and have thorough change, beneficial to mind and body alike? (Should also, in this way, gain additional time in which to install new cook, but do not put forward this rather prosaic consideration.)

Just as I think my eloquence is making headway, Robert pushes back his chair and says Well, all this is great waste of time, and he wants to get the calf off to market--which he proceeds to do.

Mademoiselle then begs for ten minutes' Serious Conversation--which I accord with outward calm and inward trepidation. The upshot of the ten minutes--which expand to seventy by the time we have done with them--is that the entire situation is more than Mademoiselle's nerves can endure, and unless she has a complete change of environment immediately, she will *succomber.*

I agree that this must at all costs be avoided, and beg her to make whatever arrangements suit her best. Mademoiselle weeps, and is still weeping when Gladys comes in to clear the breakfast things. (Cannot refrain from gloomy wonder as to nature of comments that this prolonged *tête-à-tête* will give rise to in kitchen.)

Entire morning seems to pass in these painful activities, without any definite result, except that Mademoiselle does not appear at lunch, and both children behave extraordinarily badly.

(*Mem.*: A mother's influence, if any, almost always entirely disastrous. Children invariably far worse under maternal supervision than any other.)

Resume Brittany theme with Robert once more in the evening, and suggest--stimulated by unsuccessful lunch this morning--that a Holiday Tutor might be engaged. He could, I say, swim with Robin, which would save me many qualms, and take children on expeditions. Am I, asks Robert, prepared to pay ten guineas a week for these services? Reply to this being self-evident, I do not make it, and write a letter to well-known scholastic agency.

July 29th.–Brittany practically settled, small place near Dinard selected, passports frantically looked for, discovered in improbable places, such as linen cupboard, and--in Robert's case--acting as wedge to insecurely poised chest of drawers in dressing-room--and brought up to date at considerable expense.

I hold long conversations with Travel Agency regarding hotel accommodation and registration of luggage, and also interview two holiday tutors, between whom and myself instant and violent antipathy springs up at first sight.

One of these suggests that seven and a half guineas weekly would be suitable remuneration, and informs me that he must have his evenings to himself, and the other one assures me that he is a good disciplinarian but insists upon having a Free Hand. I reply curtly that this is not what I require, and we part.

July 30th.–Wholly frightful day, entirely given up to saying good-bye to Mademoiselle. She gives us all presents, small frame composed entirely of mussel shells covered with gilt paint falling to Robert's share, and pink wool bed-socks, with four-leaved clover worked on each, to mine. We present her in return with blue leather hand-bag--into inner pocket of which I have inserted cheque--travelling clock, and small rolled-gold brooch representing crossed tennis racquets, with artificial pearl for ball--(individual effort of Robin and Vicky). All ends in emotional crescendo, culminating in floods of tears from Mademoiselle, who says nothing except *Mais voyons! Il faut se calmer*, and then weeps harder than ever. Should like to see some of this feeling displayed by children, but they remain stolid, and I explain to Mademoiselle that the reserve of the British is well known, and denotes no lack of heart, but rather the contrary.

(On thinking this over, am pretty sure that it is not in the least true--but am absolutely clear that if occasion arose again, should deliberately say the same thing.)

August 4th.–Travel to Salisbury, for express purpose of interviewing Holiday Tutor, who has himself journeyed from Reading. Terrific expenditure of time and money involved in all this makes me feel that he must at all costs be engaged--but am aware that this is irrational, and make many resolutions against foolish impetuosity.

We meet in uninspiring waiting-room, untenanted by anybody else, and I restrain myself with great difficulty from saying "Doctor Livingstone, I presume?" which would probably make him doubtful of my sanity.

Tutor looks about eighteen, but assures me that he is nearly thirty, and has been master at Prep. School in Huntingdonshire for years and years.

(*N.B.* Huntingdon most improbable-sounding, but am nearly sure that it does exist. *Mem.*: Look it up in Vicky's atlas on return home.)

Conversation leads to mutual esteem. I am gratified by the facts that he neither interrupts me every time I speak, nor assures me that he knows more about Robin than I do--(*Query:* Can he really be a schoolmaster?)–and we part cordially, with graceful assurances on my part that "I will write". Just as he departs I remember that small, but embarrassing, issue still has to be faced, and recall him in order to enquire what I owe him for to-day's expenses? He says Oh, nothing worth talking about, and then mentions a sum which appalls me. Pay it, however, without blenching, although well aware it will mean that I shall have to forgo tea in the train, owing to customary miscalculation as to amount of cash required for the day.

Consult Robert on my return; he says Do as I think best, and adds irrelevant statement about grass needing cutting, and I write to Huntingdonshire forthwith, and engage tutor to accompany us to Brittany.

Painful, and indeed despairing, reflections ensue as to relative difficulties of obtaining a tutor and a cook.

August 6th.–Mademoiselle departs, with one large trunk and eight pieces of hand luggage, including depressed-looking bouquet of marigolds, spontaneously offered by Robin. (*N.B.* Have always said, and shall continue to say, that fundamentally Robin has nicer nature than dear Vicky.) We exchange embraces; she promises to come and stay with us next summer, and says *Allons, du courage, n'est-ce pas?* and weeps again. Robert says that she will miss her train, and they depart for the station, Mademoiselle waving her handkerchief to the last, and hanging across the door at distinctly dangerous angle.

Vicky says cheerfully How soon will the Tutor arrive? and Robin picks up Helen Wills and offers to take her to see if there are any greengages--(which there cannot possibly be, as he ate the last ones, totally unripe, yesterday).

Second post brings me letter from Emma Hay, recalling Belgium--where, says Emma, I was the greatest success, underlined--which statement is not only untrue, but actually an insult to such intelligence as I may possess. She hears that I have taken a flat in London--(How?)–and is more than delighted, and there are many, many admirers of my work who will want to meet me the moment I arrive.

Am distressed at realising that although I know every word of dear Emma's letter to be entirely untrue, yet nevertheless cannot help being slightly gratified by it. Vagaries of human vanity very very curious. Cannot make up my mind in what strain to reply to Emma, so decide to postpone doing so at all for the present.

Children unusually hilarious all the evening, and am forced to conclude that loss of Mademoiselle leaves them entirely indifferent.

Read *Hatter's Castle* after they have gone to bed, and am rapidly reduced to utmost depths of gloom. Mentally compose rather eloquent letter to Book Society explaining that most of us would rather be exhilarated than depressed, although at the same time handsomely admitting that book is, as they themselves claim, undoubtedly powerful. But remember *Juan in America*–earlier choice much approved by myself--and decide to forbear. Also Robert says Do I know that it struck half-past ten five minutes ago? which I know means that he wants to put out Helen Wills, bolt front door and extinguish lights. I accordingly abandon all thoughts of eloquent letters to unknown *littérateurs* and go to bed.

August 7th.–Holiday Tutor arrives, and I immediately turn over both children to him, and immerse myself in preparations for journey, now imminent, to Brittany. At the same time, view of garden from behind bedroom window curtains permits me to ascertain that all three are amicably playing tip-and-run on lawn. This looks like auspicious beginning, and am relieved.

August 8th.–Final, and exhaustive, preparations for journey. Eleventh hour salvation descends in shape of temporary cook, offered me through telephone by Mary Kellaway, who solemnly engages to send her over one day before our return. Maids dismissed on holiday, gardener and wife solemnly adjured to Keep an Eye on the house and feed Helen Wills, and I ask tutor to sit on Robin's suitcase so that I can shut it, then forget having done so and go to store-cupboard for soap--French trains and hotels equally deficient in this commodity--and return hours later to find him still sitting there, exactly like Casabianca. Apologise profusely, am told that it does not matter, and suitcase is successfully dealt with.

Weather gets worse and worse, Shipping Forecast reduces us all to despair--(except Vicky, who says she does so hope we shall be wrecked)–and gale rises hourly. I tell Casabianca that I hope he's a good sailor; he says No, very bad indeed, and Robert suddenly announces that he can see no sense whatever in leaving home at all.

August 10th.–St. Briac achieved, at immense cost of nervous wear and tear. Casabianca invaluable in every respect, but am--rather unjustly--indignant when he informs me that he has slept all night long. History of my own night very different to this, and have further had to cope with Vicky, who does not close an eye after four A.M. and is brisk and conversational, and Robin, who becomes extremely ill from five onwards.

Land at St. Malo, in severe gale and torrents of rain, and Vicky and Robin express astonishment at hearing French spoken all round them, and Robert says that the climate reminds him of England. Casabianca says nothing, but gives valuable help with luggage and later on tells us, very nicely, that we have lost one suitcase. This causes delay, also a great deal of conversation between taxi-driver who is to take us to St. Briac, porter and unidentified friend of taxi-driver's who enters passionately into the whole affair and says fervently *Ah, grâce a Dieu!* when suitcase eventually reappears. Entire incident affords taxi-driver fund for conversation all the way to St. Briac, and he talks to us over his shoulder at frequent intervals. Robert does not seem to appreciate this, and can only hope that taxi-driver is no physiognomist, as if so, his feelings will inevitably be hurt.

We pass through several villages, and I say This must be it, to each, and nobody takes any notice except Casabianca, who is polite and simulates interest, until we finally whisk into a little *place* and stop in front of cheerful-looking Hotel with awning and little green tables outside--all dripping wet. Am concerned to notice no sign of sea anywhere, but shelve this question temporarily, in order to deal with luggage, allotment of bedrooms--(mistake has occurred here, and Madame shows cast-iron determination to treat Casabianca and myself as husband and wife)–and immediate *cafés complets* for all. These arrive, and we consume them in the hall under close and unwavering inspection of about fifteen other visitors, all British and all objectionable-looking.

Inspection of rooms ensues; Robin says When can we bathe--at which, in view of temperature, I feel myself growing rigid with apprehension--and general process of unpacking and settling in follows. Robert, during this, disappears completely, and is only recovered hours later, when he announces that The Sea is about Twenty Minutes' Walk.

General feeling prevails that I am to blame, about this, but nothing can be done, and Casabianca, after thoughtful silence, remarks that Anyway the walk will warm us. Cannot make up my mind whether this is, or is not, high example of tact. Subsequent experience, however, proves that it is totally untrue, as we all--excepting children--arrive at large and windy beach in varying degrees of chilliness. Sea is extremely green, with large and agitated waves, blown about by brisk East wind. Incredible and stupefying reflection that in less than quarter of an hour we shall be in the water--and am definitely aware that I would give quite considerable sum of money to be allowed to remain in my clothes, and on dry land. Have strong suspicion that similar frame of mind prevails elsewhere, but all cram ourselves into two bathing-huts with false assumption of joviality, and presently emerge, inadequately clad in bathing-suits.

(*N.B.* Never select blue bathing-cap again. This may be all right when circulation normal, but otherwise, effect repellent in the extreme.)

Children dash in boldly, closely followed by Holiday Tutor--to whom I mentally assign high marks for this proof of devotion to duty, as he is pea-green with cold, and obviously shivering--Robert remains on edge of sea, looking entirely superior, and I crawl with excessive reluctance into several inches of water and there become completely paralysed. Shrieks from children, who say that It is Glorious, put an end to this state of affairs, and eventually we all swim about, and tell one another that really it isn't so very cold *in* the water, but better not stay in too long on the first day.

Regain bathing-huts thankfully and am further cheered by arrival of ancient man with *eau chaude pour les pieds.*

Remainder of day devoted to excellent meals, exploring of St. Briac between terrific down-pours of rain, and purchase of biscuits, stamps, writing-pad, peaches--(very inexpensive and excellent)–and Tauchnitz volume of *Sherlock Holmes* for Robin, and *Robinson Crusoe* for Vicky.

Children eventually disposed of in bed, and Robert and Casabianca discuss appearance of our fellow-visitors with gloom and disapproval, and join in condemning me for suggesting that we should enter into conversation with all or any of them. Cannot at all admire this extremely British frame of mind, and tell them so, but go up to bed immediately before they have time to answer.

August 13th.–Opinion that St. Briac is doing us all good, definitely gaining ground. Bathing becomes less agonising, and children talk French freely with Hotel chambermaids, who are all charming. Continental breakfast unhappily not a success with Robert, who refers daily to bacon in rather embittered way, but has nothing but praise for *langoustes* and *entrecôtes* which constitute customary luncheon menu.

CONTINENTAL BREAKFAST UNHAPPILY NOT A SUCCESS WITH ROBERT

Casabianca proves admirable disciplinarian, after fearful contest with Robin concerning length of latter's stay in water. During this episode, I remain in bathing-hut, dripping wet and with one eye glued to small wooden slats through which I can see progress of affairs. Just as I am debating whether to interfere or not, Robin is vanquished, and marched out of sea with appalling calm by Casabianca. Remainder of the day wrapped in gloom, but reconciliation takes place at night, and Casabianca assures me that all will henceforward be well. (*N.B.* The young often very optimistic.)

August 15th.–I enter into conversation with two of fellow-guests at hotel, one of whom is invariably referred to by Robert as "the retired Rag-picker" owing to unfortunate appearance, suggestive of general decay. He tells me about his wife, dead years ago--(am not surprised at this)–who was, he says, a genius in her own way. Cannot find out what way was. He also adds that he himself has written books. I ask what about, and he says Psychology, but adds no more. We talk about weather--bad here, but worse in England--Wolverhampton, which he once went through and where I have never been at all--and humane slaughter, of which both of us declare ourselves to be in favour. Conversation then becomes languid, and shows a tendency to revert to weather, but am rescued by Casabianca, who says he thinks I am wanted--which sounds like the police, but is not.

Casabianca inclined to look superior, and suggest that really, the way people force their acquaintance upon one when abroad--but I decline to respond to this and tell him in return that there will be a dance at the hotel to-night and that I intend to go to it. He looks horror-stricken, and says no more.

Small problem of conduct arises here, as had no previous intention whatever of patronising dance, where I know well that Robert will flatly refuse to escort me--but do not see now how I can possibly get out of it. (*Query:* Would it be possible to compel Casabianca to act as my partner, however much against his inclination? This solution possibly undignified, but not without rather diverting aspect.)

Look for Vicky in *place*, where she habitually spends much time, playing with mongrel French dogs in gutter. Elderly English spinster--sandy-haired, and name probably Vi--tells me excitedly that some of the dogs have not been behaving quite decently, and it isn't very nice for my little girl to be with them. I reply curtly that Dogs will be Dogs, and think--too late--of many much better answers. Dogs all seem to me to be entirely respectable and well-conducted and see no reason whatever for interfering with any of them. Instead, go with Robin to grocery across the street, where we buy peaches, biscuits and bunches of small black grapes. It pours with rain, Vicky and dogs disperse, and we return indoors to play General Information in obscure corner of dining-room.

Casabianca proves distressingly competent at this, and defeats everybody, Robert included, with enquiry: "What is Wallis's line?" which eventually turns out to be connected with distinction--entirely unintelligible to me--between one form of animal life and another. Should like to send him to explain it to Vi, and see what she says--but do not, naturally, suggest this.

Children ask excessively ancient riddles, and supply the answers themselves, and Robert concentrates on arithmetical problems. Receive these in silence, and try and think of any field of knowledge in which I can hope to distinguish myself--but without success. Finally, Robin challenges me with what are Seven times Nine? to which I return brisk, but, as it turns out, incorrect, reply. Casabianca takes early opportunity of referring, though kindly, to this, and eventually suggests that half an hour's arithmetic daily would make my accounts much simpler. I accept his offer, although inwardly aware that only drastic reduction of expenditure, and improbable increase of income, could really simplify accounts--but quite agree that counting on fingers is entirely undesirable procedure, at any time of life, but more especially when early youth is past.

Bathing takes place as usual, but additional excitement is provided by sudden dramatic appearance of unknown French youth who asks us all in turns if we are doctors, as a German gentleman is having a fit in a bathing-hut. Casabianca immediately dashes into the sea--which--he declares--an English doctor has just entered. (*Query:* Is this second sight, or what?) Robin and Vicky enquire with one voice if they can go and see the German gentleman having a fit, and are with great difficulty withheld from making one dash for his bathing-cabin, already surrounded by large and excited collection.

Opinions fly about to the effect that the German gentleman is unconscious--that he has come round--that he is already dead--that he has been murdered. At this, several people scream, and a French lady says *Il ne manquait que cela!* which makes me wonder what the rest of her stay at St. Briac can possibly have been like.

Ask Robert if he does not think he ought to go and help, but he says What for? and walks away.

Casabianca returns, dripping, from the sea, followed by equally dripping stranger, presumably the doctor, and I hastily remove children from spectacle probably to be seen when bathing-hut opens; the last thing I hear being assurance from total stranger to Casabianca that he is tout *à fait aimable.*

Entire episode ends in anti-climax when Casabianca shortly afterwards returns, and informs us that The Doctor Said it was Indigestion, and the German gentleman is now walking home with his wife--who is, he adds impressively, a Norwegian. This, for reasons which continue to defy analysis, seems to add weight and respectability to whole affair.

We return to hotel, again caught in heavy shower, are besought by Robin and Vicky to stop and eat ices at revolting English tea-shop, which they patriotically prefer to infinitely superior French establishments, and weakly yield. Wind whistles through cotton frock--already wet through--that I have mistakenly put on, and Casabianca, after gazing at me thoughtfully for some moments, murmurs that I look Pale--which I think really means, Pale Mauve.

On reaching hotel, defy question of expense, and take hot bath, at cost of four francs, *prix spécial.*

Children, with much slamming of doors, and a great deal of conversation, eventually get to bed, and I say to Robert that we *might* look in at the dance after dinner--which seems easier than saying that I should like to go to it.

Robert's reply much what I expected. Eventually find myself crawling into dance-room, sideways, and sitting in severe draught, watching *le tango*, which nobody dances at all well. Casabianca, evidently feeling it his duty, reluctantly suggests that we should dance the next foxtrot--which we do, and it turns out to be Lucky Spot dance and we very nearly--but not quite--win bottle of champagne. This, though cannot say why, has extraordinarily encouraging effect, and we thereupon dance quite gaily until midnight.

August 18th.–Singular encounter takes place between Casabianca and particularly rigid and unapproachable elderly fellow-countryman in hotel, who habitually walks about in lounge wearing canary-yellow cardigan, and eyes us all with impartial dislike. Am therefore horrified when he enquires, apparently of universe at large: "What's afoot?" and Casabianca informatively replies: "Twelve inches one foot"–evidently supposing himself to be addressing customary collection of small and unintelligent schoolboys. Canary-yellow cardigan is naturally infuriated, and says that he did not get up early in the morning in order to put conundrums, or listen to their idiotic solutions--and unpleasant situation threatens.

Further discussion is, however, averted by Vicky, who falls into large open space which has suddenly appeared in floor, and becomes entangled with pipes that I hope are Gas, but much fear may be Drains. She is rescued, amongst loud cries of *Ah, pauvre petite!* and *Oh, là là!* and Casabianca removes her and says austerely that People should look where they are going. Should like to retort that People should think what they are saying--but unfortunately this only occurs to me too late.

Robert, on being told of this incident, laughs whole-heartedly for the first time since coming to St. Briac, and I reflect--as so frequently before--that masculine sense of humour is odd.

Discover that Robin is wearing last available pair of shorts, and that these are badly torn, which necessitates visit to Dinard to take white shorts to cleaners and buy material with which to patch grey ones. No one shows any eagerness to escort me on this expedition and I finally depart alone.

French gentleman with moustache occupies one side of bus and I the other, and we look at one another. Extraordinary and quite unheralded idea springs into my mind to the effect that it is definitely agreeable to find myself travelling anywhere, for any purpose, without dear Robert or either of the children. Am extremely aghast at this unnatural outbreak and try to ignore it.

(*Query:* Does not modern psychology teach that definite danger attaches to deliberate stifling of any impulse, however unhallowed? Answer probably Yes. Cannot, however, ignore the fact that even more definite danger probably attached to encouragement of unhallowed impulse. Can only conclude that peril lies in more or less every direction.)

The moustache and I look out of our respective windows, but from time to time turn round. This exercise not without a certain fascination. Should be very sorry indeed to recall in any detail peculiar fantasies that pass through my mind before Dinard is reached.

Bus stops opposite Casino, the moustache and I rise simultaneously--unfortunately bus gives a last jerk and I sit violently down again--and all is over. Final death-blow to non-existent romance is given when Robin's white shorts, now in last stages of dirt and disreputability, slide out of inadequate paper wrappings and are collected from floor by bus-conductor and returned to me.

Dinard extremely cold, and full of very unengaging trippers, most of whom have undoubtedly come from Lancashire. I deal with cleaners, packet of Lux, chocolate for children, and purchase rose-coloured bathing-cloak for myself, less because I think it suitable or becoming than because I hope it may conduce to slight degree of warmth.

Am moved by obscure feelings of remorse--(what about, in Heaven's name?)–to buy Robert a present, but can see nothing that he would not dislike immeasurably. Finally in desperation select small lump of lead, roughly shaped to resemble Napoleonic outline, and which I try to think may pass as rather unusual antique.

Do not like to omit Casabianca from this universal distribution, so purchase Tauchnitz edition of my own literary effort, but think afterwards that this is both tactless and egotistical, and wish I hadn't done it. Drink chocolate in crowded *pâtisserie*, all by myself, and surrounded by screeching strangers; am sure that French cakes used to be nicer in far-away youthful days, and feel melancholy and middle-aged. Sight of myself in glass when I powder my nose does nothing whatever to dispel any of it.

August 19th.–Robert asks if Napoleonic figure is meant for a paper-weight? I am inwardly surprised and relieved at this extremely ingenious idea, and at once say Yes, certainly. Can see by Robert's expression that he feels doubtful, but firmly change subject immediately.

Day unmarked by any particularly sensational development except that waves are even larger than usual, and twice succeed in knocking me off my feet, the last time just as I am assuring Vicky that she is perfectly safe with *me*. Robert retrieves us both from extremest depths of the ocean, and Vicky roars. Two small artificial curls--Scylla and Charybdis--always worn under bathing-cap in order that my own hair may be kept dry--are unfortunately swept away, together with bathing-cap, in this disaster, and seen no more. Bathing-cap retrieved by Casabianca, but do not like to enquire whether he cannot also pursue Scylla and Charybdis, and am accordingly obliged to return to shore without them.

(Interesting, although unprofitable, speculation comes into being here: Would not conflict between chivalry and common sense have arisen if Casabianca *had* sighted elusive side-curls, Scylla and Charybdis? What, moreover, would have been acceptable formula for returning them to me? Should much like to put this problem to him, but decide not to do so, at any rate for the present.)

August 21st.–End of stay at St. Briac approaches, and I begin to feel sentimental, but this weakness unshared by anybody else.

Loss of Scylla and Charybdis very inconvenient indeed.

August 23rd.–Am put to shame by Vicky whilst sitting outside drinking coffee on the *place* with Robert and Casabianca, fellow-guests surrounding us on every side. She bawls from an upper window that she is just going to bed, but has not kissed Casabianca good-night and would like to do so. I crane my head upwards at very uncomfortable angle and sign to her to desist, upon which she obligingly yells that To-morrow morning will *do*, and everybody looks at us. Casabianca remains unperturbed, and merely says chillingly that he Hopes she will Wash her Face first. On thinking this over, it strikes me as surely unsurpassed effort as deterrent to undesired advances, and can only trust that Vicky will not brazenly persist in path of amorous indiscretion in spite of it.

(*N.B.* Am often a prey to serious anxiety as to dear Vicky's future career. Question suggests itself: Is Success in Life incompatible with High Moral Ideals? Answer, whatever it is, more or less distressing. Can only trust that delightful scholastic establishment at Mickleham will be able to deal adequately with this problem.)

Robert shows marked tendency to say that Decent English Food again will come as a great relief, and is more cheerful than I have seen him since we left home. Take advantage of this to suggest that he and I should visit Casino at Dinard and play roulette, which may improve immediate finances, now very low, and in fact have twice had to borrow from Casabianca, without saying anything about it to Robert.

AT THE CASINO

Casino agreed upon, and we put on best clothes--which have hitherto remained folded in suitcase and extremely inadequate shelves of small wardrobe that always refuses to open.

Bus takes us to Dinard at breakneck speed, and deposits us at Casino. All is electric light, advertisement--(*Byrrh*)–and vacancy, and bartender tells us that no one will think of arriving before eleven o'clock. We have a drink each, for want of anything better to do, and sit on green velvet sofa and read advertisements. Robert asks What is *Gala des Tou-tous?* and seems disappointed when I say that I think it is little dogs. Should like--or perhaps not--to know what he thought it was.

We continue to sit on green velvet sofa, and bar-tender looks sorry for us, and turns on more electric light. This obliges us, morally, to have another drink each, which we do. I develop severe pain behind the eyes--(*Query:* Wood-alcohol, or excess of electric light?)–and feel slightly sick. Also *Byrrh* now wavering rather oddly on wall.

Robert says Well, as though he were going to make a suggestion, but evidently thinks better of it again, and nothing transpires. After what seems like several hours of this, three men with black faces and musical instruments come in, and small, shrouded heap in far corner of *salle* reveals itself as a piano.

Bar-tender, surprisingly, has yet further resources at his command in regard to electric light, and we are flooded with still greater illumination. Scene still further enlivened by arrival of very old gentleman in crumpled dress-clothes, stout woman in a green beaded dress that suggests Kensington High Street, and very young girl with cropped hair and scarlet arms. They stand in the very middle of the *salle* and look bewildered, and I feel that Robert and I are old *habitués*.

Robert says dashingly What About Another Drink? and I say No, better not, and then have one, and feel worse than ever. Look at Robert to see if he has noticed anything, and am struck by curious air about him, as of having been boiled and glazed. Cannot make up my mind whether this is, or is not, illusion produced by my own state, and feel better not to enquire, but devote entire attention to focussing *Byrrh* in spot where first sighted, instead of pursuing it all over walls and ceiling.

By the time this more or less accomplished, quite a number of people arrived, though all presenting slightly lost and *dégommé* appearance.

Robert stares at unpleasant-looking elderly man with red hair, and says Good Heavens, if that isn't old Pinkie Morrison, whom he last met in Shanghai Bar in nineteen-hundred-and-twelve. I say, Is he a friend? and Robert replies No, he never could stand the fellow, and old Pinkie Morrison is allowed to lapse once more.

Am feeling extremely ill, and obliged to say so, and Robert suggests tour of the rooms, which we accomplish in silence. Decide, by mutual consent, that we do not want to play roulette, or anything else, but would prefer to go back to bed, and Robert says he thought at the time that those drinks had something fishy about them.

I am reminded, by no means for the first time, of Edgeworthian classic, *Rosamond and the Party of Pleasure*–but literary allusions never a great success with Robert at any time, and feel sure that this is no moment for taking undue risks.

We return to St. Briac and make no further reference to evening's outing, except that Robert enquires, just as I am dropping off to sleep, whether it seems quite worth while, having spent seventy francs or so just for the sake of being poisoned and seeing a foul sight like old Pinkie Morrison? This question entirely rhetorical, and make no attempt to reply to it.

August 24th.–Much struck with extreme tact and good feeling of Casabianca at breakfast, who, after one look at Robert and myself, refrains from pressing the point as to How We enjoyed the Casino last night?

August 27th.–Last Day now definitely upon us, and much discussion as to how we are to spend it. Robert suggests Packing--but this not intended to be taken seriously--and Casabianca assures us that extremely interesting and instructive Ruins lie at a distance of less than forty kilometres, should we care to visit them. Am sorry to say that none of us *do* care to visit them, though I endeavour to palliate this by feeble and unconvincing reference to unfavourable weather.

I say what about Saint Cast, which is reputed to have admirable water-chute? or swimming-baths at Dinard? Children become uncontrollably agitated here, and say Oh, *please* can we bathe in the morning, and then come back to hotel for lunch, and bathe again in the afternoon and have tea at English Tea-Rooms? As this programme is precisely the one that we have been following daily ever since we arrived, nothing could be easier, and we agree. I make mental note to the effect that the young are definitely dependent on routine, and have dim idea of evolving interesting little article on the question, to be handsomely paid for by daily Press--but nothing comes of it.

Packing takes place, and Casabianca reminds me--kindly, but with an air of having expected rather better staff-work--that Robin's shorts are still at cleaners in Dinard. I say 0 Hell, and then weakly add -p to the end of it, and hope he hasn't noticed, and he offers to go into Dinard and fetch them. I say No, no, really, I shouldn't dream of troubling him, and he goes, but unfortunately brings back wrong parcel, from which we extract gigantic pair of white flannel trousers that have nothing to do with any of us.

French chambermaid, Germaine, who has followed entire affair from the start, says *Mon Dieu! alors c'est tout à recommencer?* which has a despairing ring, and makes me feel hopeless, but Casabianca again comes to the rescue and assures me that he can Telephone.

(*N.B.* Casabianca's weekly remuneration entirely inadequate and have desperate thoughts of doubling it on the spot, but financial considerations render this impossible, and perhaps better concentrate on repaying him four hundred francs borrowed on various occasions since arrival here.)

We go to bathe as usual, and I am accosted by strange woman in yellow pyjamas--cannot imagine how she can survive the cold--who says she met me in South Audley Street some years ago, don't I remember? Have no association whatever with South Audley Street, except choosing dinner-service there with Robert in distant days of wedding presents--(dinner service now no longer with us, and replaced by vastly inferior copy of Wedgwood). However, I say Yes, yes, of course, and yellow pyjamas at once introduces My boy at Dartmouth--very lank and mottled, and does not look me in the eye--My Sister who Has a Villa Out Here, and My Sister's Youngest Girl--Cheltenham College. Feel that I ought to do something on my side, but look round in vain, Robert, children and Casabianca all having departed, with superhuman rapidity, to extremely distant rock.

The sister with the villa says that she has read my book--ha-ha-ha--and how *do* I think of it all? I look blankly at her and say that I don't know, and feel that I am being inadequate. Everybody else evidently thinks so too, and rather distressing silence ensues, ice-cold wind--cannot say why, or from whence--suddenly rising with great violence and blowing us all to pieces.

I say Well, more feebly than ever, and yellow pyjamas says 0 dear, this weather, really--and supposes that we shall all meet down here to-morrow, and I say Yes, of course, before I remember that we cross to-night--but feel quite unable to reopen discussion, and retire to bathing-cabin.

Robert enquires later who that woman was? and I say that I cannot remember, but think her name was something like Busvine. After some thought, Robert says Was it Morton? to which I reply No, more like Chamberlain.

Hours later, remember that it was Heywood.

August 28th.–Depart from St. Briac by bus at seven o'clock, amidst much agitation. Entire personnel of hotel assembles to see us off, and Vicky kisses everybody. Robin confines himself to shaking hands quite suddenly with elderly Englishman in plus-fours--with whom he has never before exchanged a word--and elderly Englishman says that Now, doors will no longer slam on his landing every evening, he supposes. (*N.B.* Disquieting thought: does this consideration perhaps account for the enthusiasm with which we are all being despatched on our way?)

Robert counts luggage, once in French and three times in English, and I hear Casabianca--who has never of his own free will exchanged a syllable with any of his fellow-guests--replying to the retired Rag-picker's hopes of meeting again some day, with civil assent. Am slightly surprised at this.

(*Query:* Why should display of duplicity in others wear more serious aspect than similar lapse in oneself? *Answer* comes there none.)

Bus removes us from St. Briac, and we reach Dinard, and are there told that boat is *not* sailing to-night, and that we can (a) Sleep at St. Malo, (b) Remain at Dinard or (c) Return to St. Briac. All agree that this last would be intolerable anti-climax and not to be thought of, and that accommodation must be sought at Dinard.

Robert says that this is going to run us in for another ten pounds at least--which it does.

September 1st.–Home once more, and customary vicissitudes thick as leaves in Vallombrosa.

Temporary cook duly arrived, and is reasonably amiable--though soup a disappointment and strong tincture of Worcester Sauce bodes ill for general standard of cooking--but tells me that Everything was left in sad muddle, saucepans not even clean, and before she can do anything whatever will require three pudding basins, new frying-pan, fish-kettle and colander, in addition to egg-whisk, kitchen forks, and complete restocking of store-cupboard.

St. Briac hundreds of miles away already, and feel that twenty years have been added to my age and appearance since reaching home. Robert, on the other hand, looks happier.

Weather cold, and it rains in torrents. Casabianca ingenious in finding occupations for children and is also firm about proposed arithmetic lesson for myself, which takes place after lunch. Seven times table unfortunately presents difficulty that appears, so far, to be insuperable.

September 3rd.–Ask Robert if he remembers my bridesmaid, Felicity Fairmead, and he says Was that the little one with fair hair? and I say No, the very tall one with dark hair, and he says Oh yes--which does not at all convince me. Upshot of this conversation, rather strangely, is that I ask Felicity to stay, as she has been ill, and is ordered rest in the country. She replies gratefully, spare room is Turned Out--(paper lining drawer of dressing-table has to be renewed owing to last guest having omitted to screw up lip-stick securely--this probably dear Angela, but cannot be sure--and mysterious crack discovered in looking-glass, attributed--almost certainly unjustly--to Helen Wills).

I tell Casabianca at lunch that Miss Fairmead is very Musical--which is true, but has nothing to do with approaching visit, and in any case does not concern him--and he replies suitably, and shortly afterwards suggests that we should go through the Rule of Three. We do go through it, and come out the other end in more or less shattered condition. Moreover, am still definitely defeated by Seven times Eight.

September 5th.–I go up to London--Robert says, rather unnecessarily, that he supposes money is no object nowadays?–to see about the Flat. This comprises very exhausting, but interesting, sessions at furniture-shop, where I lose my head to the tune of about fifty pounds, and realise too late that dear Robert's attitude perhaps not altogether without justification.

Rose unfortunately out of town, so have to sleep at Club, and again feel guilty regarding expenditure, so dine on sausage-and-mash at Lyons establishment opposite to pallid young man who reads book mysteriously shrouded in holland cover. Feel that I must discover what this is at all costs, and conjectures waver between *The Well of Loneliness* and *The Colonel's Daughter*, until title can be spelt out upside down, when it turns out to be *Gulliver's Travels*. Distressing side-light thrown here on human nature by undeniable fact that I am distinctly disappointed by this discovery, although cannot imagine why.

In street outside I meet Viscountess once known to me in South of France, but feel doubtful if she will remember me so absorb myself passionately in shop-front, which I presently discover to be entirely filled with very peculiar appliances. Turn away again, and confront Viscountess, who remembers me perfectly, and is charming about small literary effort, which she definitely commits herself to having read. I walk with her to Ashley Gardens and tell her about the flat, which she says is the Very Thing--but does not add what for.

I say it is too late for me to come up with her, and she says Oh no, and we find lift out of order--which morally compels me to accept her invitation, as otherwise it would look as if I didn't think her worth five flights of stairs.

Am shown into beautiful fiat--first-floor Doughty Street would easily fit, lock, stock and barrel, into dining-room--and Viscountess says that the housekeeper is out, but would I like anything? I say a glass of water, please, and she is enthusiastic about the excellence of this idea, and goes out, returning, after prolonged absence, with large jug containing about an inch of water, and two odd tumblers, on a tray. I meditate writing a short article on How the Rich Live, but naturally say nothing of this aloud, and Viscountess explains that she does not know where drinking-water in the flat is obtainable, so took what was left from dinner. I make civil pretence of thinking this entirely admirable arrangement, and drink about five drops--which is all that either of us can get after equitable division of supplies. We talk about Rose, St. John Ervine and the South of France, and I add a few words about Belgium, but lay no stress on literary society encountered there.

Finally go, at eleven o'clock, and man outside Victoria Station says Good-night, girlie, but cannot view this as tribute to lingering remnant of youthful attractions as (a) it is practically pitch-dark, (b) he sounds as though he were drunk.

Return to Club bedroom and drink entire contents of water bottle.

September 6th.–Housekeeper from flat above mine in Doughty Street comes to my rescue, offers to obtain charwoman, stain floors, receive furniture and do everything else. Accept all gratefully, and take my departure with keys of flat--which makes me feel, quite unreasonably, exactly like a burglar. Should like to analyse this rather curious complex, and consider doing so in train, but all eludes me, and read *Grand Hotel* instead.

September 7th.–Felicity arrives, looking ill. (*Query:* Why is this by no means unbecoming to her, whereas my own afflictions invariably entail mud-coloured complexion, immense accumulation of already only-too-visible lines on face, and complete limpness of hair?) She is, as usual, charming to the children--does not tell them they have grown, or ask Robin how he likes school, and scores immediate success with both.

I ask what she likes for dinner--(should be indeed out of countenance if she suggested anything except chicken, sardines or tinned corn, which so far as I know is all we have in the house)–and she says An Egg. And what about breakfast to-morrow morning? She says An Egg again, and adds in a desperate way that an egg is all she wants for any meal, ever.

Send Vicky to the farm with a message about quantity of eggs to be supplied daily for the present.

Felicity lies down to rest, and I sit on windowsill and talk to her. We remind one another of extraordinary, and now practically incredible, incidents in bygone schooldays, and laugh a good deal, and I feel temporarily younger and better-looking.

Remember with relief that Felicity is amongst the few of my friends that Robert *does* like, and evening passes agreeably with wireless and conversation. Suggest a picnic for to-morrow--at which Robert says firmly that he is obliged to spend entire day in Plymouth--and tie knot in handkerchief to remind myself that cook must be told jam sandwiches, not cucumber. Take Felicity to her room, and hope that she has enough blankets--if not, nothing can be easier than to produce others without any trouble whatever--Well, in that case, says Felicity, perhaps--Go to linen-cupboard and can find nothing there whatever except immense quantities of embroidered tea-cloths, unhealthy-looking pillow oozing feathers, and torn roller-towel. Go to Robin's bed, but find him wide-awake, and quite impervious to suggestion that he does not *really* want more than one blanket on his bed, so have recourse to Vicky, who is asleep. Remove blanket, find it is the only one and replace it, and finally take blanket off my own bed, and put in on Felicity's, where it does not fit, and has to be tucked in till mattress resembles a valley between two hills. Express hope--which sounds ironical--that she may sleep well, and leave her.

September 8th.–Our Vicar's Wife calls in the middle of the morning, in deep distress because no one can be found to act as producer in forthcoming Drama Competition. Will I be an angel? I say firmly No, not on this occasion, and am not sure that Our Vicar's Wife does not, on the whole, look faintly relieved. But what, I ask, about herself? No--Our Vicar has put his foot down. Mothers' Union, Women's Institute, G.F.S. and Choir Outings by all means--but one evening in the week must and shall be kept clear. Our Vicar's Wife, says Our Vicar, is destroying herself, and this he cannot allow. Quite feel that the case, put like this, is unanswerable.

Our Vicar's Wife then says that she knows the very person--excellent actress, experienced producer, willing to come without fee. Unfortunately, is now living at Melbourne, Australia. Later on she also remembers other, equally talented, acquaintances, one of whom can now never leave home on account of invalid husband, the other of whom died just eleven months ago.

I feel that we are getting no further, but Our Vicar's Wife says that it has been a great relief to talk it all over, and perhaps after all she can persuade Our Vicar to let her take it on, and we thereupon part affectionately.

September 10th.–Picnic, put off on several occasions owing to weather, now takes place, but is--like so many entertainments--rather qualified success, partly owing to extremely mountainous character of spot selected. Felicity shows gallant determination to make the best of this, and only begs to be allowed to take her own time, to which we all agree, and divide rugs, baskets, cushions, thermos flasks and cameras amongst ourselves. Ascent appears to me to take hours, moreover am agitated about Felicity, who seems to be turning a rather sinister pale blue colour. Children full of zeal and activity, and dash on ahead, leaving trail of things dropped on the way. Casabianca, practically invisible beneath two rugs, mackintosh and heaviest basket, recalls them, at which Robin looks murderous, and Vicky feigns complete deafness, and disappears over the horizon.

Question as to whether we shall sit in the sun or out of the sun arises, and gives rise to much amiable unselfishness, but is finally settled by abrupt disappearance of sun behind heavy clouds, where it remains. Felicity sits down and pants, but is less blue. I point out scenery, which constitutes only possible excuse for having brought her to such heights, and she is appreciative. Discover that sugar has been left behind. Children suggest having tea at once, but are told that it is only four o'clock, and they had better explore first. This results in Robin's climbing a tree, and taking *Pickwick Papers* out of his pocket to read, and Vicky lying flat on her back in the path, and chewing blades of grass. Customary caution as to unhygienic properties peculiar to blades of grass ensues, and I wonder--not for the first time--why parents continue to repeat admonitions to which children never have paid, and never will pay, slightest attention. Am inspired by this reflection to observe suddenly to Felicity that, anyway, I'm glad my children aren't *prigs*–at which she looks startled, and says, Certainly not--far from it--but perceive that she has not in any way followed my train of thought--which is in no way surprising.

We talk about Italy, the Book Society--*Red Ike* a fearful mistake, but *The Forge* good--and how can Mr. Hugh Walpole find time for all that reading, and write his own books as well--and then again revert to far-distant schooldays, and ask one another what became of that girl with the eyes, who had a father in Patagonia, and if anybody ever heard any more of the black satin woman who taught dancing the last year we were there?

Casabianca, who alone has obeyed injunction to explore, returns, followed by unknown black-and-white dog, between whom and Vicky boisterous and ecstatic friendship instantly springs into being--and I unpack baskets, main contents of which appear to be bottles of lemonade--at which Felicity again reverts to paleblueness--and pink sugar-biscuits. Can only hope that children enjoy their meal.

Customary feelings of chill, cramp and general discomfort invade me--feel certain that they have long ago invaded Felicity, although she makes no complaint--and picnic is declared to be at an end. Black-and-white dog remains glued to Vicky's heels, is sternly dealt with by Casabianca, and finally disappears into the bracken, but at intervals during descent of hill, makes dramatic reappearances, leaping up in attitudes reminiscent of ballet-dancing. Owners of dog discovered at foot of hill, large gentleman in brown boots, and very thin woman with spats and eye-glasses.

Vicky is demonstrative with dog, the large gentleman looks touched, and the eye-glasses beg my pardon, but if my little girl has really taken a fancy to the doggie, why, they are looking for a home for him--just off to Zanzibar--otherwise, he will have to be destroyed. I say Thank you, thank you, we really couldn't think of such a thing, and Vicky screams and ejaculates.

The upshot of it all is that we *do* think of such a thing--Casabianca lets me down badly, and backs up Vicky--the large gentleman says Dog may not be one of these pedigree animals--which I can see for myself he isn't--but has no vice, and thoroughly good-natured and affectionate--and Felicity, at whom I look, nods twice--am reminded of Lord Burleigh, but do not know why--and mutters *Oui, oui, pourquoi pas?*–which she appears to think will be unintelligible to anyone except herself and me.

Final result is that Vicky, Robin and dog occupy most of the car on the way home, and I try and make up my mind how dog can best be introduced to Robert and Cook.

September 11th.–Decision reached--but cannot say how--that dog is to be kept, and that his name is to be Kolynos.

September 12th.–All is overshadowed by National Crisis, and terrific pronouncements regarding income-tax and need for economy. Our Vicar goes so far as to talk about the Pound from the pulpit, and Robert is asked by Felicity to explain the whole thing to her after dinner--which he very wisely refuses to do.

We lunch with the Frobishers, who are depressed, and say that the wages of everyone on the Estate will have to be reduced by ten per cent. (*Query:* Why are they to be sympathised with on this account? Am much sorrier for their employés.)

Young Frobisher, who is down from Oxford, says that he has seen it coming for a long while now. (Should like to know why, in that case, he did not warn the neighbourhood.) He undertakes to make all clear--this, once more, at Felicity's request--and involved monologue follows, in which the Pound, as usual, figures extensively. Am absolutely no wiser at the end of it all than I was at the beginning and feel rather inclined to say so, but Lady F. offers me coffee, and asks after children--whom she refers to as "the boy and that dear little Virginia"–and we sink into domesticities and leave the Pound to others. Result is that it overshadows the entire evening and is talked about by Felicity and Robert all the way home in very learned but despondent strain.

(*N.B.* A very long while since I have heard Robert so eloquent, and am impressed by the fact that it takes a National Crisis to rouse him, and begin to wish that own conversational energies had not been dissipated for years on such utterly unworthy topics as usually call them forth. Can see dim outline of rather powerful article here, or possibly viers fibres more suitable form--but nothing can be done to-night.) Suggest hot milk to Felicity, who looks cold, take infinite trouble to procure this, but saucepan boils over and all is wasted.

September 13th.–Curious and regrettable conviction comes over me that Sunday in the country is entirely intolerable. Cannot, however, do anything about it.

Kolynos chases Helen Wills up small oak-tree, and eats arm and one ear off teddy-bear owned by Vicky. This not a success, and Robert says tersely that if the dog is going to do *that* kind of thing--and then leaves the sentence unfinished, which alarms us all much more than anything he could have said.

ROBIN SINGING IN CHURCH

Am absent-minded in Church, but recalled by Robin singing hymn, entirely out of tune, and half a bar in advance of everybody else. Do not like to check evident zeal, and feel that this should come within Casabianca's province, but he takes no notice. (*Query:* Perhaps he, like Robin, has no ear for music? He invariably whistles out of tune.)

Return to roast beef--underdone--and plates not hot. I say boldly that I think roast beef every Sunday is a mistake--why not chicken, or even mutton? but at this everyone looks aghast, and Robert asks What next, in Heaven's name? so feel it better to abandon subject, and talk about the Pound, now familiar topic in every circle.

General stupor descends upon Robert soon after lunch, and he retires to study with *Blackwood's Magazine.* Robin reads *Punch*; Vicky, amidst customary protests, disappears for customary rest; and Casabianca is nowhere to be seen. Have strong suspicion that he has followed Vicky's example.

I tell Felicity that I *must* write some letters, and she rejoins that so must she, and we talk until twenty minutes to four, and then say that it doesn't really matter, as letters wouldn't have gone till Monday anyhow. (This argument specious at the moment, but has very little substance when looked at in cold blood.)

Chilly supper--only redeeming feature, baked potatoes--concludes evening, together with more talk of the Pound, about which Robert and Casabianca become, later on, technical and masculine, and Felicity and I prove unable to stay the course, and have recourse to piano instead.

Final peak of desolation is attained when Felicity, going to bed, wishes to know why I have so completely given up my music, and whether it isn't a Great Pity?

Point out to her that all wives and mothers always *do* give up their music, to which she agrees sadly, and we part without enthusiasm.

Should be very sorry to put on record train of thought aroused in me by proceedings of entire day.

September 15th.–End of holidays, as usual, suddenly reveal themselves as being much nearer than anyone had supposed, and Cash's Initials assume extraordinary prominence in scheme of daily life, together with School Lists, new boots for Robin, new everything for Vicky, and tooth-paste for both.

This all dealt with, more or less, after driving Felicity to station, where we all part from her with regret. Train moves out of station just as I realise that egg sandwiches promised her for journey have been forgotten. Am overcome with utterly futile shame and despair, but can do nothing. Children sympathetic, until distracted by man on wheels--Stop me and Buy One--which they do, to the extent of fourpence. Should be prepared to take my oath that far more than fourpenny-worth of ice-cream will subsequently be found in car and on their clothes.

Extraordinarily crowded morning concluded with visit to dentist, who says that Vicky is Coming Along Nicely, and that Robin can be Polished Off Now, and offers, on behalf of myself, to have a look round, to which I agree, with unsatisfactory results. Look at this! says dentist unreasonably. *Look* at it! Waving in the Wind! Object strongly to this expression, which I consider gross exaggeration, but cannot deny that tooth in question is not all it should be. Much probing and tapping follows, and operator finally puts it to me--on the whole very kindly and with consideration--that this is a Question of Extraction. I resign myself to extraction accordingly, and appoint a date after the children have gone to school.

(Have often wondered to what extent mothers, if left to themselves, would carry universal instinct for putting off everything in the world until after children have gone to school? Feel certain that this law would, if it were possible, embrace everything in life, death itself included.)

It is too late to go home to lunch, and we eat fried fish, chipped potatoes, galantine and banana splits in familiar café.

September 20th.–Suggest to Robert that the moment has now come for making use of Doughty Street flat. I can take Vicky to London, escort her from thence to Mickleham, and then settle down in flat. Settle down what to? says Robert. Writing, I suggest weakly, and seeing Literary Agent. Robert looks unconvinced, but resigned. I make arrangements accordingly.

Aunt Gertrude writes to say that sending a little thing of Vicky's age right away from home is not only unnatural, but absolutely wrong. Have I, she wants to know, any idea of what a childless home will be like? Decide to leave this letter unanswered, but am disgusted to find that I mentally compose at least twelve different replies in the course of the day, each one more sarcastic than the last. Do not commit any of them to paper, but am just as much distracted by them as if I had--and have moments, moreover, of regretting that Aunt Gertrude will never know all the things I *might* have said.

Vicky, whom I observe anxiously, remains unmoved and cheerful, and refers constantly and pleasantly to this being her Last Evening at home. Moreover, pillow remains bone-dry, and she goes peacefully to sleep rather earlier than usual.

September 22nd.–Robin is taken away by car, and Casabianca escorts Vicky and myself to London, and parts from us at Paddington. I make graceful speech, which I have prepared beforehand, about our gratitude, and hope that he will return to us at Christmas. (Am half inclined to add, if state of the Pound permits--but do not like to.) He says, Not at all, to the first part, and Nothing that he would like better, to the second, and makes a speech on his own account. Vicky embraces him with ardour and at some length, and he departs, and Vicky immediately says Now am I going to school? Nothing is left but to drive with her to Waterloo and thence to Mickleham, where Vicky is charmingly received by Principal, and made over to care of most engaging young creature of seventeen, introduced as Jane. Fearful inclination to tears comes over me, but Principal is tact personified, and provides tea at exactly right moment. She promises, unprompted, to telephone in the morning, and write long letter next day, and Vicky is called to say good-bye, which she does most affectionately, and with undiminished radiance.

September 25th.–Doughty Street.–Quite incredibly, find myself more or less established, and startlingly independent. Flat--once I have bought electric fire, and had it installed by talkative young man with red hair--very comfortable; except for absence of really restful arm-chair, and unfamiliarity of geyser-bath, of which I am terrified. Bathroom is situated on stairs, which are in continual use, and am therefore unable to take bath with door wide open, as I should like to do. Compromise with open window, through which blacks come in, and smell of gas and immense quantities of steam, go out. Remainder of steam has strange property of gathering itself on to the ceiling and there collecting, whence it descends upon my head and shoulders in extraordinarily cold drops. Feel sure that there is scientific, and doubtless interesting, explanation of this minor chemical phenomenon, but cannot at the moment work it out. (*N.B.* Keep discussion of this problem for suitable occasion, preferably when seated next to distinguished scientist at dinner-party. In the meantime, cower beneath bath towel in farthest corner of bathroom--which is saying very little--but am quite unable to dodge unwanted shower-bath.)

Housekeeper from flat above extremely kind and helpful, and tells me all about arrangements for window-cleaning, collecting of laundry and delivery of milk.

Excellent reports reach me of Vicky at Mickleham--Robin writes--as usual--about unknown boy called Felton who has brought back a new pencil-box this term, and other, equally unknown, boy whose parents have become possessed of house in the New Forest--and Robert sends laconic, but cheerful, account of preparations for Harvest Home supper. Less satisfactory communication arrives from Bank, rather ungenerously pointing out extremely small and recent overdraft. This almost incredible, in view of recent unexpected literary gains, and had felt joyfully certain of never again finding myself in this painful position--but now perceive this to have been wholly unjustifiable optimism. (Material for short philosophic treatise on vanity of human hopes surely indicated here? but on second thoughts, too reminiscent of Mr. Fairchild, so shall leave it alone.)

Write quantities of letters, and am agreeably surprised at immense advantage to be derived from doing so without any interruptions.

September 27th.–Rose telephones to ask if I would like to come to literary evening party, to be given by distinguished novelist whose books are well known to me, and who lives in Bloomsbury. I say Yes, if she is sure it will be All Right. Rose replies Why not, and then adds--distinct afterthought--that I am myself a Literary Asset to society, nowadays. Pause that ensues in conversation makes it painfully evident that both of us know the last statement to be untrue, and I shortly afterwards ring off.

I consider the question of what to wear, and decide that black is dowdy, but green brocade with Ciro pearls will be more or less all right, and shall have to have old white satin shoes recovered to match.

September 28th.–Literary party, to which Rose takes me as promised. Take endless trouble with appearance, and am convinced, before leaving flat, that this has reached very high level indeed, thanks to expensive shampoo-and-set, and moderate use of cosmetics. Am obliged to add, however, that on reaching party and seeing everybody else, at once realise that I am older, less well dressed, and immeasurably plainer than any other woman in the room. (Have frequently observed similar reactions in myself before.)

Rose introduces me to hostess--she looks much as I expected, but photographs which have appeared in Press evidently, and naturally, slightly idealised. Hostess says how glad she is that

I was able to come--(*Query:* Why?)–and is then claimed by other arrivals, to whom she says exactly the same thing, with precisely similar intonation. (*Note:* Society of fellow-creatures promotes cynicism. Should it be avoided on this account? If so, what becomes of Doughty Street flat?)

THE PARTY IN BLOOMSBURY

Rose says Do I see that man over there? Yes, I do. He has written a book that will, says Rose impressively, undoubtedly be seized before publication and burnt. I enquire how she knows, but she is claimed by an acquaintance and I am left to gaze at the man in silent astonishment and awe. Just as I reach the conclusion that he cannot possibly be more than eighteen years old, I hear a scream--this method of attracting attention absolutely unavoidable, owing to number of people all talking at once--and am confronted by Emma I lay in rose-coloured fishnet, gold lace, jewelled turban and necklace of large barbaric pebbles.

Who, shrieks Emma, would have dreamt of this? and do I see that man over there? He has just finished a book that is to be seized and burnt before publication. A genius, of course, she adds casually, but far in advance of his time. I say Yes, I suppose so, and ask to be told who else is here, and Emma gives me rapid outline of many rather lurid careers, leading me to conclusion that literary ability and domestic success not usually compatible. (*Query:* Will this invalidate my chances?)

Dear Emma then exclaims that It is Too Bad I should be so utterly Out of It--which I think might have been better worded--and introduces a man to me, who in his turn introduces his wife, very fair and pretty. (Have unworthy spasm of resentment at sight of so much attractiveness, but stifle instantly.) Man offers to get me a drink, I accept, he offers to get his wife one, she agrees, and he struggles away through dense crowd. Wife points out to me young gentleman who has written a book that is to be seized, etc., etc. Am disgusted to hear myself saying in reply Oh really, in tone of intelligent astonishment.

Man returns with two glasses of yellow liquid--mine tastes very nasty, and wife leaves hers unfinished after one sip--and we talk about Income Tax, the Pound, France, and John van Druten, of whom we think well. Rose emerges temporarily from press of distinguished talkers, asks Am I all right, and is submerged again before I can do more than nod. (Implied lie here.) Man and his wife, who do not know anyone present, remain firmly glued to my side, and I to theirs for precisely similar reason. Conversation flags, and my throat feels extremely sore. Impossibility of keeping the Pound out of the conversation more and more apparent, and character of the observations that we make about it distinguished neither for originality nor for sound constructive quality.

Emma recrudesces later, in order to tell me that James--(totally unknown to me) has at last chucked Sylvia--(of whom I have never heard)–and is definitely living with Naomi--(again a complete blank)–who will have to earn enough for both, and for her three children--but James' children by Susan are being looked after by dear Arthur. I say, without conviction, that this at least is a comfort, and Emma--turban now definitely over right eyebrow--vanishes again.

Original couple introduced by Emma still my sole hope of companionship, and am morally certain that I am theirs. Nevertheless am quite unable to contemplate resuming analysis of the Pound, which I see looming ahead, and am seriously thinking of saying that there is a man here whose book is to be seized prior to publication, when Rose intervenes, and proposes departure. Our hostess quite undiscoverable, Emma offers officious and extremely scandalous explanation of this disappearance, and Rose and I are put into taxi by elderly man, unknown to me, but whom I take to be friend of Rose's, until she tells me subsequently that she has never set eyes on him in her life before. I suggest that he may be man-servant hired for the occasion, but Rose says No, more likely a distinguished dramatist from the suburbs.

October 1st.–Direct result of literary party is that I am rung up on telephone by Emma, who says that she did not see anything like enough of me and we must have a long talk, what about dinner together next week in Soho where she knows of a cheap place? (This, surely, rather odd form of invitation?) Am also rung up by Viscountess's secretary, which makes me feel important, and asked to lunch at extremely expensive and fashionable French restaurant. Accept graciously, and spend some time wondering whether circumstances would justify purchase of new hat for the occasion. Effect of new hat on *morale* very beneficial, as a rule.

Also receive letter--mauve envelope with silver cipher staggers me from the start--which turns out to be from Pamela Pringle, who is mine affectionately as ever, and is so delighted to think of my being in London, and *must* talk over dear old days, so will I ring her up immediately and suggest something? I do ring her up--although not immediately--and am told that she can just fit me in between massage at four and Bridge at six, if I will come round to her flat in Sloane Street like an angel. This I am willing to do, but make mental reservation to the effect that dear old days had better remain in oblivion until P. P. herself introduces them into conversation, which I feel certain she will do sooner or later.

Proceed in due course to flat in Sloane Street--entrance impressive, with platoons of hall-porters, one of whom takes me up in lift and leaves me in front of bright purple door with antique knocker representing mermaid, which I think unsuitable for London, although perhaps applicable to Pamela's career. Interior of flat entirely furnished with looking-glass tables, black pouffes, and acutely angular blocks of green wood. Am over-awed, and wonder what Our Vicar's Wife would feel about it all--but imagination jibs.

Pamela receives me in small room--more looking-glass, but fewer pouffes, and angular blocks are red with blue zigzags--and startles me by kissing me with utmost effusion. This very kind, and only wish I had been expecting it, as could then have responded better and with less appearance of astonishment amounting to alarm. She invites me to sit on a pouffe and smoke a Russian cigarette, and I do both, and ask after her children. Oh, says Pamela, the *children!* and begins to cry, but leaves off before I have had time to feel sorry for her, and bursts into long and complicated speech. Life, declares Pamela, is very, *very* difficult, and she is perfectly certain that I feel, as she does, that nothing in the world matters except Love. Stifle strong inclination to reply that banking account, sound teeth and adequate servants matter a great deal more, and say Yes Yes, and look as intelligently sympathetic as possible.

Pamela then rushes into impassioned speech, and says that It is not her fault that men have always gone mad about her, and no doubt I remember that it has always been the same, ever since she was a mere tot--(do not remember anything of the kind, and if I did, should certainly not say so)–and that after all, divorce is not looked upon as it used to be, and it's always the woman that has to pay the penalty, don't I agree? Feel it unnecessary to make any very definite reply to this, and am in any case not clear as to whether I do agree or not, so again have recourse to air of intelligent understanding, and inarticulate, but I hope expressive, sound. Pamela apparently completely satisfied with this, as she goes on to further revelations to which I listen with eyes nearly dropping out of my head with excitement. Stevenson, Templer-Tate, Pringle, are all referred to, as well as others whose names have not actually been borne by Pamela--but this, according to her own account, her fault rather than theirs. Feel I ought to say something, so enquire tentatively if her first marriage was a happy one--which sounds better than asking if *any* of her marriages were happy ones. *Happy?* says Pamela. Good Heavens, what am I talking about? Conclude from this, that it was *not* a happy one. Then what, I suggest, about Templer-Tate? That, Pamela replies sombrely, was Hell. (Should like to enquire for whom, but do not, naturally, do so.) Next branch of the subject is presumably Pringle, and here I again hesitate, but Pamela takes initiative and long and frightful story is poured out.

Waddell--such is Pringle's Christian name, which rouses in me interesting train of speculative thought as to mentality of his parents--Waddell does not understand his wife. Never has understood her, never possibly could understand her. She is sensitive, affectionate, intelligent in her own way though of course not *clever*, says Pamela--and really, although she says so herself, remarkably easy to get on with. A Strong Man could have done anything in the world with her. She is like that. The ivy type. Clinging. I nod, to show agreement. Further conversation reveals that she has clung in the wrong directions, and that this has been, and is being, resented by Pringle. Painful domestic imbroglio is unfolded. I say weakly that I am sorry to hear this--which is not true, as I am thoroughly enjoying myself--and ask what about the children? This brings us back to the beginning again, and we traverse much ground that has been gone over before. Bridge at six is apparently forgotten, and feel that it might sound unsympathetic to refer to it, especially when Pamela assures me that she very, very often thinks of Ending it All. Am not sure if she means life altogether, or only life with Pringle--or perhaps just present rather irregular course of conduct?

Telephone-calls five times interrupt us, when Pamela is effusive and excitable to five unknown conversationalists and undertakes to meet someone on Friday at three, to go and see someone else who is being too, too ill in a Nursing Home, and to help somebody else to meet a woman who knows someone who is connected with films.

Finally, take my leave, after being once more embraced by Pamela, and am shot down in lift--full of looking-glass, and am much struck with the inadequacy of my appearance in these surroundings, and feel certain that lift-attendant is also struck by it, although aware that his opinion ought to be matter of complete indifference to me.

Temperature of Sloane Street seems icy after interior of flat, and cold wind causes my nose to turn scarlet and my eyes to water. Fate selects this moment for the emergence of Lady B.–sable furs up to her eyebrows and paint and powder unimpaired--from Truslove and Hanson, to waiting car and chauffeur. She sees me and screams--at which passers-by look at us, astonished--and says Good gracious her, what next? She would as soon have expected to see the geraniums from the garden uprooting themselves from the soil and coming to London. (Can this be subtle allusion to effect of the wind upon my complexion?) I say stiffly that I am staying at My Flat for a week or two. Where? demands Lady B. sceptically--to which I reply, Doughty Street, and she shakes her head and says that conveys *nothing*. Should like to refer her sharply to *Life of Charles Dickens*, but before I have time to do so she asks what on earth I am doing in Sloane

Street, of all places--I say, spending an hour or two with my old friend Pamela Pringle--(for which I shall later despise myself, as should never have dreamt of referring to her as anything of the kind to anybody else). Oh, *that* woman, says Lady B., and offers to give me a lift to Brondesbury or wherever-it-is, as her chauffeur is quite brilliant at knowing his way *anywhere.* Thank her curtly and refuse. We part, and I wait for a 19 bus and wish I'd told Lady B. that I *must* hurry, or should arrive late for dinner at Apsley House.

October 3rd.–Observe in myself tendency to go further and further in search of suitable cheap restaurants for meals--this not so much from economic considerations, as on extremely unworthy grounds that walking in the streets amuses me. (Cannot for one instant contemplate even remote possibility of Lady B.'s ever coming to hear of this, and do not even feel disposed to discuss it with Robert. Am, moreover, perfectly well aware that I have come to London to Write, and not to amuse myself.)

THE BLOOMSBURY TEA SHOP

Determination to curb this spirit causes me to lunch at small establishment in Theobald's Road, completely filled by hatless young women with cigarettes, one old lady with revolting little dog that growls at everyone, and small, pale youth who eats custard, and reads mysterious periodical entitled *Helping Hands.*

Solitary waitress looks harassed, and tells me--unsolicited--that she has only a small portion of The Cold left. I say Very Well, and The Cold, after long interval, appears, and turns out to be pork. Should like to ask for a potato, but waitress avoids me, and I go without.

Hatless young women all drink coffee in immense quantities, and I feel this is literary, and should like to do the same, but for cast-iron conviction that coffee will be nasty. Am also quite unattracted by custard, and finally ask for A Bun, please, and waitress--more harassed than ever--enquires in return if I mind the one in the window? I recklessly say No, if it hasn't been there too long, and waitress says Oh, not very, and seems relieved.

Singular conversation between hatless young women engages my attention, and distracts me from rather severe struggle with the bun. My neighbours discuss Life, and the youngest of them remarks that Perversion has practically gone out altogether now. The others seem to view this as pessimistic, and assure her encouragingly that, so far, nothing else has been found to take its place. One of them adjures her to Look at Sprott and Nash--which sounds like suburban grocers, but is, I think, mutual friends. Everybody says Oh, of course, to Sprott and Nash, and seems relieved. Someone tells a story about a very old man, which I try without success to overhear, and someone else remarks disapprovingly that *he* can't know much about it, really, as he's well over seventy and it only came into fashion a year or two ago. Conversation then becomes inconsequent, and veers about between *Cavalcade*, methods of hair-dressing, dog-breeding, and man called William--but with tendency to revert at intervals to Sprott and Nash.

Finish bun with great difficulty, pay tenpence for entire meal, leave twopence for waitress, and take my departure. Decide quite definitely that this, even in the cause of economy, wasn't worth it. Remember with immense satisfaction that I lunch to-morrow at Boulestin's with charming Viscountess, and indulge in reflections concerning strange contrasts offered by Life: cold pork and stale bun in Theobald's Road on Tuesday, and lobster and *poire Hélène*–(I hope)–at Boulestin's on Wednesday. Hope and believe with all my heart that similar startling, dissimilarity will be observable in nature of company and conversation.

Decide to spend afternoon in writing and devote much time to sharpening pencils, looking for india-rubber--finally discovered inside small cavity of gramophone, intended for gramophone needles. This starts train of thought concerning whereabouts of gramophone needles, am impelled to search for them, and am eventually dumbfounded at finding them in a match-box, on shelf of kitchen cupboard. (Vague, but unpleasant, flight of fancy here, beginning with Vicky searching for biscuits in insufficient light, and ending in Coroner's Court and vote of severe censure passed--rightly--by Jury.)

(*Query:* Does not imagination, although in many ways a Blessing, sometimes carry its possessor too far? *Answer* emphatically Yes.) Bell rings, and I open door to exhausted-seeming woman, who says she isn't going to disturb me--which she has already done--but do I know about the new electric cleaner? I feel sorry for her, and feel that if I turn her away she will very likely break down altogether, so hear about new electric cleaner, and engage, reluctantly, to let it come and demonstrate its powers to-morrow morning. Woman says that I shall never regret it--which is untrue, as I am regretting it already--and passes out of my life.

Second interruption takes place when man--says he is Unemployed--comes to the door with a Poem, which he says he is selling. I buy the Poem for two shillings, which I know is weak, and say that he really must not send anyone else as I cannot afford it. He assures me that he never will, and goes.

Bell rings again, and fails to leave off. I am filled with horror, and look up at it--inaccessible position, and nothing to be seen except two mysterious little jam-jars and some wires. Climb on a chair to investigate, then fear electrocution and climb down again without having done anything. Housekeeper from upstairs rushes down, and unknown females from basement rush up, and we all look at the ceiling and say Better fetch a Man. This is eventually done, and I meditate ironical article on Feminism, while bell rings on madly. Man, however, arrives, says Ah, yes, he thought as much, and at once reduces bell to order, apparently by sheer power of masculinity.

Am annoyed, and cannot settle down to anything.

October 7th. Extraordinary behaviour of dear Rose, with whom I am engaged--and have been for days past--to go and have supper tonight. Just as I am trying to decide whether bus to

Portland Street or tube to Oxford Circus will be preferable, I am called up on telephone by Rose's married niece, who lives in Hertfordshire, and is young and modern, to say that speaker for her Women's Institute to-night has failed, and that Rose, on being appealed to, has at once suggested my name and expressed complete willingness to dispense with my society for the evening. Utter impossibility of pleading previous engagement is obvious; I contemplate for an instant saying that I have influenza, but remember in time that niece, very intelligently, started the conversation by asking how I was, and that I replied Splendid, thanks--and there is nothing for it but to agree.

(*Query:* Should much like to know if it was for this that I left Devonshire.)

Think out several short, but sharply worded, letters to Rose, but time fails; I can only put brush and comb, slippers, sponge, three books, pyjamas and hot-water bottle into case--discover later that I have forgotten powder-puff, and am very angry, but to no avail--and repair by train to Hertfordshire.

Spend most of journey in remembering all that I know of Rose's niece, which is that she is well under thirty, pretty, talented, tremendous social success, amazingly good at games, dancing, and--I think--everything else in the world, and married to brilliantly clever young man who is said to have Made Himself a Name, though cannot at the moment recollect how.

Have strong impulse to turn straight round and go home again, sooner than confront so much efficiency, but non-stop train renders this course impracticable.

Niece meets me--clothes immensely superior to anything that I ever have had, or shall have--is charming, expresses gratitude, and asks what I am going to speak about. I reply, Amateur Theatricals. Excellent, of course, she says unconvincingly, and adds that the Institute has a large Dramatic Society already, that they are regularly produced by well-known professional actor, husband of Vice-President, and were very well placed in recent village-drama competition, open to all England.

At this I naturally wilt altogether, and say Then perhaps better talk about books or something--which sounds weak, even as I say it, and am convinced that niece feels the same, though she remains imperturbably charming. She drives competently through the night, negotiates awkward entrance to garage equally well, extracts my bag and says that It is Heavy--which is undeniable, and is owing to books, but cannot say so, as it would look as though I thought her house likely to be inadequately supplied--and conducts me into perfectly delightful, entirely modern, house, which I feel certain--rightly, I discover later--has every newest labour-saving device ever invented.

Bathroom especially--(all appears to be solid marble, black-and-white tiles, and dazzling polish)–impresses me immeasurably. Think regretfully, but with undiminished affection, of extremely inferior edition at home--paint peeling in several directions, brass taps turning green at intervals until treated by housemaid, and irregular collection of home-made brackets on walls, bearing terrific accumulation of half-empty bottles, tins of talcum powder and packets of Lux.

Niece shows me her children--charming small boy, angelic baby--both, needless to say, have curls. She asks civilly about Robin and Vicky, and I can think of nothing whatever to the credit of either, so merely reply that they are at school.

N.B. Victorian theory as to maternal pride now utterly discredited. Affection, yes. Pride, no.

We have dinner--niece has changed into blue frock which suits her and is, of course, exactly right for the occasion. I do the best I can with old red dress and small red cap that succeeds in being thoroughly unbecoming without looking in the least up to date, and endeavour to make wretched little compact from bag do duty for missing powder-puff. Results not good.

We have a meal, am introduced to husband--also young--and we talk about Rose, mutual friends, *Time and Tide* and Electrolux cleaners.

Evening at Institute reasonably successful--am much impressed by further display of efficiency from niece, as President--I speak about Books, and obtain laughs by introduction of three entirely irrelevant anecdotes, am introduced to felt hat and fur coat, felt hat and blue jumper, felt hat and tweeds, and so on. Names of all alike remain impenetrably mysterious, as mine no doubt to them.

(Flight of fancy here as to whether this deplorable, but customary, state of affairs is in reality unavoidable? Theory exists that it has been completely overcome in America, where introductions always entirely audible and frequently accompanied by short biographical sketch. Should like to go to America.)

Niece asks kindly if I am tired. I say No not at all, which is a lie, and she presently takes me home and I go to bed. Spare-room admirable in every respect, but no waste-paper basket. This solitary flaw in general perfection a positive relief.

October 8th.–All endeavours to communicate with Rose by telephone foiled, as her housekeeper invariably answers, and says that she is Out. Can quite understand this. Resolve that dignified course is to take no further steps, and leave any advances to Rose.

This resolution sets up serious conflict later in day, when I lunch with Viscountess, originally met as Rose's friend, as she does nothing but talk of her with great enthusiasm, and I am torn between natural inclination to respond and sense of definite grievance at Rose's present behaviour.

Lunch otherwise highly successful. Have *not* bought new hat, which is as well, as Viscountess removes hers at an early stage, and is evidently quite indifferent to millinery.

October 10th.–Am exercised over minor domestic problem, of peculiarly prosaic description, centering round collection of Dust-bins in small, so-called back garden of Doughty Street flat. All these dust-bins invariably brim-full, and am convinced that contents of alien waste-paper baskets contribute constantly to mine, as have no recollection at all of banana-skin, broken blue-and-white saucer, torn fragments of *Police-Court Gazette*, or small, rusty tin kettle riddled with holes.

Contemplate these phenomena with great dislike, but cannot bring myself to remove them, so poke my contribution down with handle of feather-duster, and retire.

October 13th.–Call upon Rose, in rather unusual frame of mind which suddenly descends upon me after lunch--cannot at all say why--impelling me to demand explanation of strange behaviour last week.

Rose at home, and says How nice to see me, which takes the wind out of my sails, but I rally, and say firmly that That is All Very Well, but what about that evening at the Women's Institute? At this Rose, though holding her ground, blanches perceptibly, and tells me to sit down quietly and explain what I mean. Am very angry at *quietly*, which sounds as if I usually smashed up all the furniture, and reply--rather scathingly--that I will do my best not to rouse the neighbourhood. Unfortunately, rather unguarded movement of annoyance results in upsetting of small table, idiotically loaded with weighty books, insecurely fastened box of cigarettes, and two ash-trays. We collect them again in silence--cigarettes particularly elusive, and roll to immense distances underneath sofa and behind electric fire--and finally achieve an arm-chair apiece, and glare at one another across expanse of Persian rug.

Am astonished that Rose is able to look me in the face at all, and say so, and long and painful conversation ensues, revealing curious inability on both our parts to keep to main issue. Should be sorry to recall in any detail exact number and nature of utterly irrelevant observations exchanged, but have distinct recollection that Rose asserts at various times that: (a) If I had been properly psycho-analysed years ago, I should realise that my mind has never really come to maturity at all. (b) It is perfectly ridiculous to wear shoes with such high heels. (c) Robert is a perfect *saint* and has a lot to put up with. (d) No one in the world can be readier than Rose is to admit that I can Write, but to talk about The Piano is absurd.

Cannot deny that in return I inform her, in the course of the evening, that: (a) Her best friend could never call Rose tidy--look at the room now! (b) There is a great difference between being merely impulsive, and being utterly and grossly inconsiderate. (c) Having been to America does not, in itself, constitute any claim to infallibility on every question under the sun. (d) Naturally, what's past is past, and I don't want to remind her about the time she lost her temper over those idiotic iris-roots.

Cannot say at what stage I am reduced to tears, but this unfortunately happens, and I explain that it is entirely due to rage, and nothing else. Rose suddenly says that there is nothing like coffee, and rings the bell. Retire to the bathroom in great disorder, mop myself up--tears highly unbecoming, and should much like to know how film-stars do it, usual explanation of Glycerine seems to me quite inadequate--Return to sitting-room and find that Rose, with extraordinary presence of mind, has put on the gramophone. Listen in silence to Rhapsody in Blue, and feel better.

Admirable coffee is brought in, drink some, and feel better still. Am once more enabled to meet Rose's eye, which now indicates contrition, and we simultaneously say that this is Perfectly Impossible, and Don't let's quarrel, whatever we do. All is harmony in a moment, and I kiss Rose, and she says that the whole thing was her fault, from start to finish, and I say No, it was mine *absolutely*, and we both say that we didn't really mean anything we said.

(Cold-blooded and slightly cynical idea crosses my mind later that entire evening has been complete waste of nervous energy, if neither of us meant any of the things we said--but refuse to dwell on this aspect of the case.)

Eventually go home feeling extraordinarily tired. Find letter from Vicky, with small drawing of an elephant, that I think distinctly clever and modernistic, until I read letter and learn that it is A Table, laid for Dinner, also communication from Literary Agent saying how much he looks forward to seeing my new manuscript. (Can only hope that he enjoys the pleasures of anticipation as much as he says, since they are, at present rate of progress, likely to be prolonged.)

Am also confronted by purple envelope and silver cypher, now becoming familiar, and scrawled invitation from Pamela Pringle to lunch at her flat, and meet half a dozen dear friends who simply adore my writing. Am sceptical about this, but shall accept, from degraded motives of curiosity to see the dear friends, and still more degraded motives of economy, leading me to accept a free meal from whatever quarter offered.

October 16th.–Find myself in very singular position as regards the Bank, where distinctly unsympathetic attitude prevails in regard to quite small overdraft. Am interviewed by the Manager, who says he very much regrets that my account at present appears to be absolutely *Stationary*. I say with some warmth that he cannot regret it nearly as much as I do myself, and dead-lock appears to have been reached. Manager--cannot imagine why he thinks it a good idea--suddenly opens a large file, and reads me out extract from correspondence with very unendearing personality referred to as his Director, instructing him to bring pressure to bear upon this client--(me). I say Well, that's all right, he *has* brought pressure to bear, so he needn't worry--but perfect understanding fails to establish itself, and we part in gloom.

Idle fantasy of suddenly acquiring several hundreds of thousands of pounds by means of Irish Sweep ticket nearly causes me to be run over by inferior-looking lorry with coal.

October 18th.–Go to Woolworth's to buy paper handkerchiefs--cold definitely impending--and hear excellent sixpenny record, entitled "Around the Corner and Under the Tree", which I buy. Tune completely engaging, and words definitely vulgar, but not without cheap appeal.

Something tells me that sooner or later I shall be explaining purchase away by saying that I got it to amuse the children.

(*Note:* Self-knowledge possibly beneficial, but almost always unpleasant to a degree.)

Determine to stifle impending cold, if only till after Pamela's luncheon-party to-morrow, and take infinite trouble to collect jug, boiling water, small bottle of Friar's Balsam and large bath-towel. All is ruined by one careless movement, which tips jug, Friar's Balsam and hot water down front of my pyjamas. Am definitely scalded--skin breaks in one place and turns scarlet over area of at least six inches--try to show presence of mind and remember that Butter is The Thing, remember that there is no butter in the flat--frantic and irrelevant quotation here, *It was the Best butter*–remember vaseline, use it recklessly, and retire to bed in considerable pain and with cold unalleviated.

October 19th.–Vagaries of Fate very curious and inexplicable. Why should severe cold in the head assail me exactly when due to lunch with Pamela Pringle in character of reasonably successful authoress, in order to meet unknown gathering of smart Society Women? Answer remains impenetrably mysterious.

Take endless trouble with appearance, decide to wear my Blue, then take it all off again and revert to my Check, but find that this makes me look like a Swiss nursery governess, and return once more to Blue. Regret, not for the first time, that Fur Coat, which constitutes my highest claim to distinction of appearance, will necessarily have to be discarded in hall.

Sloane Street achieved, as usual, via bus No. 19, and I again confront splendours of Pamela's purple front door. Am shown into empty drawing-room, where I meditate in silence on unpleasant, but all-too-applicable, maxim that It is Provincial to Arrive too Early. Presently strange woman in black, with colossal emerald brooch pinned in expensive-looking frills of lace, is shown in, and says How d'y do, very amiably, and we talk about the weather, Gandhi and French poodles. (Why? There are none in the room, and can trace no association of ideas whatsoever.)

Two more strange women in black appear, and I feel that my Blue is becoming conspicuous. All appear to know one another well, and to have met last week at lunch, yesterday evening at Bridge, and this morning at an Art Exhibition: No one makes any reference to Pamela, and grave and unreasonable panic suddenly assails me that I am in wrong flat altogether. Look madly round to see if I can recognise any of the furniture, and woman with osprey and rope of pearls enquires if I am missing that *precious* horse. I say No, not really--which is purest truth--and wonder if she has gone off her head. Subsequent conversation reveals that horse was made of soapstone.

(*Query:* What is soapstone? Association here with Lord Darling, but cannot work out in full.)

More and more anxious about non-appearance of Pamela P., especially when three more guests arrive--black two-piece, black coat-and-skirt, and black crêpe-de-chine with orange-varnished nails. (My Blue now definitely revealed as inferior imitation of Joseph's coat, no less, and of very nearly equal antiquity.)

They all call one another by Christian names, and have much to say about mutual friends, none of whom I have ever heard of before. Someone called Goo-goo has had influenza, and while this is being discussed, I am impelled to violent sneezing fit. Everybody looks at me in horror, and conversation suffers severe check.

(*Note:* Optimistic conviction that two handkerchiefs will last out through one luncheon party utterly unjustified in present circumstances. Never forget this again.)

Door flies open and Pamela Pringle, of whom I have now given up all hope, rushes in, kisses everybody, falls over little dog--which has mysteriously appeared out of the blue and vanishes again after being fallen over--and says Oh do we all know one another, and isn't she a *fearfully* bad hostess but she simply could *not* get away from Amédé, who really is a Pet. (Just as I have decided that Amédé is another little dog, it turns out that he is a Hairdresser.)

Lunch is announced, and we all show customary reluctance to walking out of the room in simple and straightforward fashion, and cluster round the threshold with self-depreciating expressions until herded out by Pamela. I find myself sitting next to her--quite undeserved position of distinction, and probably intended for somebody else--with extraordinarily elegant black crêpe-de-chine on other side.

Black crepe-de-chine says that she adored my book, and so did her husband, and her sister-in-law, who is Clever and never says *Anything* unless she really Means It, thought it quite marvellous. Having got this off her chest, she immediately begins to talk about recent visit of her own to Paris, and am forced to the conclusion that her standards of sincerity must fall definitely below those of unknown sister-in-law.

Try to pretend that I know Paris as well as she does, but can see that she is not in the least taken in by this.

Pamela says Oh, *did* she see Georges in Paris, and what are the new models like? but crêpe-de-chine shakes her head and says Not out yet, and Georges never will show any Spring things before December, at very earliest--which to me sounds reasonable, but everybody else appears to feel injured about it, and Pamela announces that she sometimes thinks seriously about letting Gaston make for her instead of Georges--which causes frightful sensation. Try my best to look as much startled and horrified as everybody else, which is easy as am certain that I am about to sneeze again--which I do.

(Both handkerchiefs now definitely soaked through and through, and sore will be out on upper lip before day is over.)

Conversation veers about between Paris, weight-reduction--(quite unnecessary, none of them can possibly weigh more than seven stone, if that)–and annexation by someone called Diana of second husband of someone else called Tetsie, which everyone agrees was *utterly* justified, but no reason definitely given for this, except that Tetsie is a perfect *darling*, we all know, but no one on earth could possibly call her smartly turned-out.

(Feel that Tetsie and I would have at least one thing in common, which is more than I can say about anybody else in the room--but this frame of mind verging on the sardonic, and not to be encouraged.)

Pamela turns to me just as we embark on entirely admirable *coupe Jacques*, and talks about books, none of which have been published for more than five minutes and none of which, in consequence, I have as yet read--but feel that I am expected to be on my own ground here, and must--like Mrs. Dombey--make an effort, which I do by the help of remembering Literary Criticisms in *Time and Tide*'s issue of yesterday.

Interesting little problem hovers on threshold of consciousness here: How on earth do Pamela and her friends achieve conversation about books which I am perfectly certain they have none of them read? Answer, at the moment, baffles me completely.

Return to drawing-room ensues; I sneeze again, but discover that extreme left-hand corner of second pocket handkerchief is still comparatively dry, which affords temporary, but distinct, consolation.

On the whole, am definitely relieved when emerald-brooch owner says that It is too, too sad, but she must fly, as she really is responsible for the whole thing, and it can't begin without her--which might mean a new Permanent Wave, or a command performance at Buckingham Palace, but shall never now know which, as she departs without further explanation.

Make very inferior exit of my own, being quite unable to think of any reason for going except that I have been wanting to almost ever since I arrived,–which cannot, naturally, be produced. Pamela declares that having me has been Quite Wonderful, and we part.

Go straight home and to bed, and Housekeeper from upstairs most kindly brings me hot tea and cinnamon, which are far too welcome for me to make enquiry that conscience prompts, as to their rightful ownership.

October 23rd.–Telephone bell rings at extraordinary hour of eleven-eighteen P.M., and extremely agitated voice says Oh is that me, to which I return affirmative answer and rather curt rider to the effect that I have been in bed for some little while. Voice then reveals itself as belonging to Pamela P.–which doesn't surprise me in the least--who is, she says, in great, great trouble, which she cannot possibly explain. (Should much like to ask whether it was worth while getting me out of bed in order to hear that no explanation is available.) But, Pamela asks, will I, whatever happens, *swear* that she has spent the evening with me, in my flat? If I will not do this, then it is--once more--perfectly impossible to say what will happen. But Pamela knows that I will--I always was a darling--and I couldn't refuse such a tiny, tiny thing, which is simply a question of life and death.

Am utterly stunned by all this, and try to gain time by enquiring weakly if Pamela can by any chance tell me where she really *has* spent the evening? Realise as soon as I have spoken that this is not a tactful question, and am not surprised when muffled scream vibrates down receiver into my ear. Well, never mind *that*, then, I say, but just give me some idea as to who is likely to ask me what Pamela's movements have been, and why. Oh, replies Pamela, she is the most absolutely misunderstood woman on earth, and don't I feel that men are simply brutes? There isn't one of them--not one--whom one can trust to be really tolerant and broad-minded and understanding. They only want One Thing.

Feel quite unable to cope with this over telephone wire, and am, moreover, getting cold, and find attention straying towards possibility of reaching switch of electric fire with one hand whilst holding receiver with the other. Flexibility of the human frame very remarkable, but cannot altogether achieve this and very nearly overbalance, but recover in time to hear Pamela saying that if I will do this one thing for her, she will never, never forget it. There isn't anyone else, she adds, whom she *could* ask. (Am not at all sure if this is any compliment.) Very well, I reply, if asked, I am prepared to say that Pamela spent the evening with me here, but I hope that no one *will* ask and Pamela must distinctly understand that this is the first and last time I shall ever do anything of the kind. Pamela begins to be effusive, but austere voice from the unseen says that Three Minutes is Up, will we have another Three, to which we both say No simultaneously, and silence abruptly supervenes.

Crawl into bed again feeling exactly as if I had been lashed to an iceberg and then dragged at the cart's tail. Very singular and unpleasant sensation. Spend disturbed and uncomfortable night, evolving distressing chain of circumstances by which I may yet find myself at the Old Bailey committing perjury and--still worse--being found out--and, alternatively, imagining that I hear rings and knocks at front door, heralding arrival of Pamela P.'s husband bent on extracting information concerning his wife's whereabouts.

Wake up, after uneasy dozings, with bad headache, impaired complexion and strong sensation of guilt. Latter affects me to such a degree that am quite startled and conscience-stricken at receiving innocent and childlike letters from Robin and Vicky, and am inclined to write back and say that they ought not to associate with me--but breakfast restores balance, and I resolve to relegate entire episode to oblivion. (*Mem.*: Vanity of human resolutions exemplified here, as I find myself going over and over telephone conversation all day long, and continually inventing admirable exhortations from myself to Pamela P.)

Robert writes briefly, but adds P.S. Isn't it time that I thought about coming home again? which I think means that he is missing me, and feel slightly exhilarated.

October 25th.–Am taken out to lunch by Literary Agent, which makes me feel important, and celebrated writers are pointed out to me--mostly very disappointing, but must on no account judge by appearances. Literary Agent says Oh, by the way, he has a small cheque for me at the office, shall he send it along? Try to emulate this casualness, and reply Yes, he may as well, and shortly afterwards rush home and write to inform Bank Manager that, reference our recent conversation, he may shortly expect to receive a Remittance--which I think sounds well, and commits me to nothing definite.

October 27th.–Am chilled by reply from Bank Manager, who has merely Received my letter and Noted Contents. This lack of *abandon* very discouraging, moreover very different degree of eloquence prevails when subject under discussion is deficit, instead of credit, and have serious thoughts of writing to point this out.

Receive curious and unexpected tribute from total stranger in the middle of Piccadilly Circus, where I have negotiated crossing with success, but pause on refuge, when voice says in my ear that owner has been following me ever since we left the pavement--which does, indeed, seem like hours ago--and would like to do so until Haymarket is safely reached. Look round at battered-looking lady carrying three parcels, two library books, small umbrella and one glove, and say Yes, yes, certainly, at the same time wondering if she realises extraordinarily insecure foundations on which she has built so much trust. Shortly afterwards I plunge, Look Right, Look Left, and execute other manoeuvres, and find myself safe on opposite side. Battered-looking lady has, rather to my horror, disappeared completely, and I see her no more. Must add this to life's many other unsolved mysteries.

THE BATTERED LADY (p. 164)

Meanwhile, select new coat and skirt--off the peg, but excellent fit, with attractive black suede belt--try on at least eighteen hats--very, very aggravating assistant who tells me that I look Marvellous in each, which we both know very well that I don't--and finally select one with a brim--which is not, says the assistant, being worn at all now, but after all, there's no telling when they may come in again--and send Robert small jar of *pâté de foie gras* from Jackson's in Piccadilly.

October 31st.–Letters again give me serious cause for reflection. Robert definitely commits himself to wishing that I would come home again, and says--rather touchingly--that he finds one can see the house from a hill near Plymouth, and he would like me to have a look at it. Shall never wholly understand advantages to be derived from seeing any place from immense distance instead of close at hand, as could so easily be done from the tennis lawn without any exertion at all--but quite realise that masculine point of view on this question, as on so many others, differs from my own, and am deeply gratified by dear Robert's thought of me.

Our Vicar's Wife sends post card of Lincoln Cathedral, and hopes on the back of it that I have not forgotten our Monthly Meeting on Thursday week, and it seems a long time since I left home, but she hopes I am enjoying myself and has no time for more as post just going, and if I am anywhere near St. Paul's Churchyard, I might just pop into a little bookseller's at the corner of a little courtyard somewhere quite near the Cathedral, and see if they are doing anything about Our Vicar's little pamphlet, of which they had several copies in the summer. But I am not to take *any* trouble about this, on any account. Also, across the top of post card, could I just look in at John Barker's, when I happen to be anywhere near, and ask the price of filet lace there? But not to put myself out, in any way. Robert, she adds across top of address, seems *very lonely*, underlined, also three exclamation marks, which presumably denote astonishment. Why?

November 2nd.–Regretfully observe in myself cynical absence of surprise when interesting invitations pour in on me just as I definitely decide to leave London and return home. Shall not, however, permit anything to interfere with date appointed and undertaking already given by Robert on half-sheet of note-paper, to meet 4.1 8 train at local station next Tuesday.

Buy two dust-sheets--yellow-and-white check, very cheap--with which to swathe furniture of fiat during my absence. Shopman looks doubtful and says Will two be all I require, and I say Yes, I have plenty of others. Absolute and gratuitous lie, which covers me with shame when I think of it afterwards.

November 3rd.–Further telephone communication from Pamela P., but this time of a less sensational character, as she merely says that the fog makes her feel too, too suicidal, and she's had a fearful run of bad luck at Bridge and lost twenty-three pounds in two afternoons, and don't I feel that when things have got to *that* stage there's nothing for it but a complete change? To this I return with great conviction Oh, absolutely *nothing*, and mentally frame witty addition to the effect that after finding myself unplaced in annual whist-drive in our village, I always make a point of dashing over the Somerset border. This quip, however, joins so many others in limbo of the unspoken.

I ask Pamela where she is going for complete change and she astonishes me by replying Oh, the Bahamas. That is, if Waddell agrees, but so far he is being difficult, and urging the Pyrenees. I say weakly Well, wouldn't the Pyrenees be very nice in their own way?–but Pamela, to this, exclaims My dear! in shocked accents, and evidently thinks less than nothing of the Pyrenees. The fact is, she adds, that she has a *very* great friend in the Bahamas, and he terribly wants her to come out there, and really things are so dreadfully complicated in London that she sometimes feels the only thing to do is to GO. (This I can well believe, but still think the Bahamas excessive.) Meanwhile, however, have I a free afternoon because Pamela has heard of a really marvellous clairvoyante, and she wants someone she can really *trust* to go there with her, only not one word about it to Waddell, ever. Should like to reply to this that I now take it for granted that any activity of Pamela's is subject to similar condition--but instead say that I should like to come to marvellous clairvoyante, and am prepared to consult her on my own account. All is accordingly arranged, including invitation from myself to Pamela to lunch with me at my Club beforehand, which she effusively agrees to do.

Spend the rest of the afternoon wishing that I hadn't asked her.

November 6th.–Altogether unprecedented afternoon, with Pamela Pringle. Lunch at my Club not an unmitigated success, as it turns out that Pamela is slimming and can eat nothing that is on menu and drink only orangeade, but she is amiable whilst I deal with chicken casserole and pineapple flan, and tells me about a really wonderful man--(who knows about wild beasts)–who has adored her for years and years, absolutely without a thought of self. Exactly like something in a book, says Pamela. She had a letter from him this morning, and do I think it's fair to go on writing to him? If there is one thing that Pamela never has been, never possibly could be, it is the kind of woman who Leads a Man On. Lead, kindly Light, I say absently, and then feel I have been profane as well as unsympathetic, but Pamela evidently not hurt by this as she pays no attention to it whatever and goes on to tell me about brilliant man-friend in the Diplomatic Service, who telephoned from The Hague this morning and is coming over next week by air apparently entirely in order that he may take Pamela out to dine and dance at the Berkeley.

Anti-climax supervenes here whilst I pay for lunch and conduct Pamela to small and crowded dressing-room, where she applies orange lipstick and leaves her rings on wash-stand and has to go back for them after taxi has been called and is waiting outside.

Just as I think we are off page-boy dashes up and says Is it Mrs. Pringle, she is wanted on the telephone, and Pamela again rushes. Ten minutes later she returns and says Will I forgive her, she gave this number as a very great friend wanted to ring her up at lunch-time, and in Sloane Street flat the telephone is often so difficult, not that there's anything to conceal, but people get such queer ideas, and Pamela has a perfect horror of things being misunderstood. I say that I can quite believe it, then think this sounds unkind, but on the whole do not regret having said it.

Obscure street in Soho is reached, taxi dismissed after receiving vast sum from Pamela, who insists on paying, and we ascend extraordinarily dirty stairs to second floor, where strong smell of gas prevails. Pamela says Do I think it's all right? I reply with more spirit than sincerity, that of course it is, and we enter and are received by anaemic-looking young man with curls, who takes one look at us and immediately vanishes behind green plush curtain, but reappears, and says that Madame Inez is quite ready but can only receive one client at a time. Am not surprised when Pamela compels me to go first, but give her a look which I hope she understands is not one of admiration.

Interview with unpleasant-looking sibyl follows. She gazes into large glass ball and says that I have known grief--(should like to ask her who hasn't)–and that I am a wife and a mother. Juxtaposition of these statements no doubt unintentional. Long and apparently inspired monologue follows, but little of practical value emerges except that: (a) There is trouble in the near future. (If another change of cook, this is definitely unnerving.) (b) I have a child whose name will one day be famous. (Reference here almost certainly to dear Vicky.) (c) In three years' time I am to cut loose from my moorings, break new ground and throw my cap over the windmill.

THE VISIT TO THE FORTUNE TELLER

None of it sounds to me probable, and I thank her and make way for Pamela. Lengthy wait ensues, and I distinctly hear Pamela scream at least three times from behind curtain. Finally she emerges in great agitation, throws pound notes about, and tells me to Come away quickly--which we both do, like murderers, and hurl ourselves into first available taxi quite breathless.

Pamela shows disposition to clutch me and weep, and says that Madame Inez has told her she is a reincarnation of Helen of Troy and that there will never be peace in her life. (Could have told her the last part myself, without requiring fee for doing so.) She also adds that Madame Inez predicts that Love will shortly enter into her life on hitherto unprecedented scale, and alter it completely--at which I am aghast, and suggest that we should both go and have tea somewhere at once.

We do so, and it further transpires that Pamela did not like what Madame Inez told her about the past. This I can well believe.

We part in Sloane Street, and I go back to fiat and spend much time packing.

November 7th.–Doughty Street left behind, yellow-and-white dust-sheets amply sufficing for entire flat, and Robert meets me at station. He seems pleased to see me but says little until seated in drawing-room after dinner, when he suddenly remarks that He has Missed Me. Am astonished and delighted, and should like him to enlarge on theme, but this he does not do, and we revert to wireless and *The Times*.

* * * * *

April 13th.–Immense and inexplicable lapse of time since diary last received my attention, but on reviewing past five months, can trace no unusual activities, excepting arrears of calls--worked off between January and March on fine afternoons, when there appears to be reasonable chance of finding everybody out--and unsuccessful endeavour to learn cooking by correspondence in twelve lessons.

Financial situation definitely tense, and inopportune arrival of Rates casts a gloom, but Robert points out that they are not due until May 28th, and am unreasonably relieved. *Query:* Why? *Reply* suggests, not for the first time, analogy with Mr. Micawber.

April 15th.–Felicity Fairmead writes that she *could* come for a few days' visit, if we can have her, and may she let me know exact train later, and it will be either the 18th or the 19th, but, if inconvenient, she could make it the 27th, only in that case, she would have to come by Southern Railway and *not* G.W.R. I write back five pages to say that this would be delightful, only not the 27th, as Robert has to take the car to Crediton that day, and any train that suits her best, of course, but Southern easiest for us.

Have foreboding that this is only the beginning of lengthy correspondence and number of extremely involved arrangements. This fear confirmed by telegram received at midday from Felicity: Cancel letter posted yesterday could after all come on twenty-first if convenient writing suggestions to-night.

Say nothing to Robert about this, but unfortunately fresh telegram arrives over the telephone, and is taken down by him, to the effect that Felicity is So sorry but plans altered Writing.

Robert makes no comment, but goes off at seven o'clock to a British Legion Meeting, and does not return till midnight. Casablanca and I have dinner *tête-à-tête*, and talk about dog-breeding, the novels of E. F. Benson, and the Church of England, about which he holds to my mind optimistic views. Just as we retire to the drawing-room and wireless, Robin appears in pyjamas, and says that he has distinctly heard a burglar outside his window.

I give him an orange--but avoid Casabianca's eye, which is disapproving--and after short sessions by the fire, Robin departs and no more is heard about burglar. Drawing-room, in the most extraordinary way, smells of orange for the rest of the evening to uttermost corners of the room.

April 19th.–Felicity not yet here, but correspondence continues briskly, and have given up telling Robert anything about which train he will be required to meet.

Receive agreeable letter from well-known woman writer, personally unknown to me, who says that We have Many Friends in Common, and will I come over to lunch next week and bring anyone I like with me? Am flattered, and accept for self and Felicity. (*Mem.*: Notify Felicity on post card of privilege in store for her, as this may help her to decide plans.) Further correspondence consists of Account Rendered from Messrs. Frippy and Coleman, very curtly worded, and far more elaborate epistle, which fears that it has escaped my memory, and ventures to draw my attention to enclosed, also typewritten notice concerning approaching Jumble Sale--(about which I know a good deal already, having contributed two hats, three suspender-belts, disintegrating fire-guard, and a foot-stool with Moth)–and request for reference of last cook but two.

Weather very cold and rainy, and daily discussion takes place between Casabianca and children as to desirability or otherwise of A Walk. Compromise finally reached with Robin and Vicky each wheeling a bicycle uphill, and riding it down, whilst Casabianca, shrouded in mackintosh to the eyebrows, walks gloomily in the rear, in unrelieved solitude. Am distressed at viewing this unnatural state of affairs from the window, and meditate appeal to Robin's better feelings, if any, but shall waste no eloquence upon Vicky.

Stray number of weekly Illustrated Paper appears in hall--cannot say why or how--and Robert asks where this rag came from? and then spends an hour after lunch glued to its pages. Paper subsequently reaches the hands of Vicky, who says Oh, look at that picture of a naked lady, and screams with laughter. Ascertain later that this description, not wholly libellous, applies to full-page photograph of Pamela Pringle--wearing enormous feathered headdress, jewelled breast-plates, one garter, and a short gauze skirt--representing Chastity at recent Pageant of Virtue through the Ages organised by Society women for the benefit of Zenana Mission.

PAMELA PRINGLE AS "CHASTITY"

I ask Robert, with satirical intent, if he would like me to take in Illustrated Weekly regularly, to which he disconcerts me by replying Yes, but not that one. He wants the one that Marsh writes in. Marsh? I say. Yes, Marsh. Marsh is a sound fellow, and knows about books. That, says Robert, should appeal to me. I agree that it does, but cannot, for the moment, trace Marsh. Quite brisk discussion ensues, Robert affirming that I know all about Marsh--everyone does--fellow who writes regularly once a week about books. Illumination suddenly descends upon me, and I exclaim, Oh, Richard King! Robert signifies assent, and adds that he knew very well that I knew about the fellow, everyone does--and goes into the garden.

(*Mem.*: Wifely intuition very peculiar and interesting, and apparently subject to laws at present quite unapprehended by finite mind. Material here for very deep, possibly scientific, article. Should like to make preliminary notes, but laundry calls, and concentrate instead on total omission of everything except thirty-four handkerchiefs and one face-towel from clothes-basket. Decide to postpone article until after the holidays.)

Ethel's afternoon out, and customary fatality of callers ensues, who are shown in by Cook with unsuitable formula: Someone to see you, 'm. Someone turns out to be unknown Mrs. Poppington, returning call with quite unholy promptitude, and newly grown-up daughter, referred to as My Girl. Mrs. Poppington sits on window-seat--from which I hastily remove Teddy-bear, plasticine, and two pieces of bitten chocolate--and My Girl leans back in arm-chair and reads *Punch* from start to finish of visit.

Mrs. P. and I talk about servants, cold East Winds and clipped yew hedges. She also says hopefully that she thinks I know Yorkshire, but to this I have to reply that I don't, which leads us nowhere. Am unfortunately inspired to add feebly--Except, of course, the Brontes--at which Mrs. P. looks alarmed, and at once takes her leave. My Girl throws *Punch* away disdainfully, and we exchange good-byes, Mrs. P. saying fondly that she is sure she does not know what I must think of My Girl's manners. Could easily inform her, and am much tempted to do so, but My Girl at once starts engine of car, and drives herself and parent away.

April 21st.–Final spate of letters, two post cards, and a telegram, herald arrival of Felicity--not, however, by train that she has indicated, and minus luggage, for which Robert is obliged to return to station later. Am gratified to observe that in spite of this, Robert appears pleased to see her, and make mental note to the effect that a Breath of Air from the Great World is of advantage to those living in the country.

April 22nd.–Singular reaction of Felicity to announcement that I am taking her to lunch with novelist, famous in two continents for numerous and brilliant contributions to literature. It is very kind of me, says Felicity, in very unconvincing accents, but should I mind if she stayed at home with the children? I should, I reply, mind very much indeed. At this we glare at one another for some moments in silence, after which Felicity--spirit evidently quailing--mutters successively that: (a) She has no clothes. (b) She won't know what to talk about. (c) She doesn't want to be put into a book.

I treat (a) and (b) with silent contempt, and tell her that (c) is quite out of the question, to which she retorts sharply that she doesn't know what I mean.

Dead-lock is again reached.

Discussion finally closed by my declaring that Casabianca and the children are going to Plymouth to see the dentist, and that Robert will be out, and I have told the maids that there will he no dining-room lunch. Felicity submits, I at once offer to relinquish expedition altogether, she protests violently, and we separate to go and dress.

Query, at this point, suggests itself: Why does my wardrobe never contain anything except heavy garments suitable for arctic regions, or else extraordinarily flimsy ones suggestive of the tropics? Golden mean apparently non-existent.

Am obliged to do the best I can with brown tweed coat and skirt, yellow wool jumper--sleeves extremely uncomfortable underneath coat sleeves--yellow handkerchief tied in artistic sailor's knot at throat, and brown straw hat with ciré ribbon, that looks too summery for remainder of outfit. Felicity achieves better results with charming black-and-white check, short pony-skin jacket, and becoming black felt hat.

Car, which has been washed for the occasion, is obligingly brought to the door by Casabianca, who informs me that he does not think the self-starter is working, but she will probably go on a slope, only he doesn't advise me to try and wind her, as she kicked badly just now. General impression diffused by this speech is to the effect that we are dealing with a dangerous wild beast rather than a decrepit motor-car.

I say Thank you to Casabianca, Good-bye to the children, start the car, and immediately stop the engine. Not a very good beginning, is it? says Felicity, quite unnecessarily.

STARTING THE CAR

Casabianca, Robin and Vicky, with better feeling, push car vigorously, and eventually get it into the lane, when engine starts again. Quarter of a mile further on, Felicity informs me that she thinks one of the children is hanging on to the back of the car. I stop, investigate, and discover Robin, to whom I speak severely. He looks abashed. I relent, and say, Well, never mind this time, at which he recovers immediately, and waves us off with many smiles from the top of a hedge.

Conversation is brisk for the first ten miles. Felicity enquires after That odious woman--cannot remember her name--but she wore a ridiculous cape, and read books, from which description I immediately, and correctly, deduce Miss Pankerton, and reply that I have not, Thank Heaven, come across her for weeks. We also discuss summer clothes, Felicity's married sister's children, Lady B.–now yachting in the Mediterranean--and distant days when Felicity and I were at school together.

Pause presently ensues, and Felicity--in totally different voice--wishes to know if we are nearly there? We are; I stop the car before the turning so that we can powder our noses, and we attain small and beautiful Queen Anne house in silence.

Am by this time almost as paralysed as Felicity, and cannot understand why I ever undertook expedition at all. Leave car in most remote corner of exquisite courtyard--where it presents peculiarly sordid and degraded appearance--and permit elegant parlourmaid--mauve-and-white dress and mob cap--to conduct us through panelled hall to sitting-room evidently designed and furnished entirely regardless of cost.

Madam is in the garden, says parlourmaid, and departs in search of her. Felicity says to me, in French--(Why not English?)–*Dites que je ne suis pas* literary *du tout*, and I nod violently just as celebrated hostess makes her appearance.

She is kind and voluble; Felicity and I gradually recover; someone in a blue dress and pince-nez appears, and is introduced as My Friend Miss Postman who Lives with Me; someone else materialises as My Cousin Miss Crump, and we all go in to lunch. I sit next to hostess, who talks competently about modern poetry, and receives brief and evasive replies from myself. Felicity has My Friend Miss Postman, whom I hear opening the conversation rather unfortunately with amiable remark that she has so much enjoyed Felicity's book. Should like to hear with exactly what energetic turn of phrase Felicity disclaims having had anything to do with any book ever, but cannot achieve this, being under necessity of myself saying something reasonably convincing about Masefield, about whose work I can remember nothing at all.

Hostess then talks about her own books, My Friend Miss Postman supplies intelligent and laudatory comments, seconded by myself, and Felicity and the cousin remain silent, but wear interested expressions.

This carries us on safely to coffee in the *loggia*, where Felicity suddenly blossoms into brilliancy owing to knowing names, both Latin and English, of every shrub and plant within sight.

She is then taken round the garden at great length by our hostess, with whom she talks gardening. Miss P. and I follow, but ignore flora, and Miss P. tells me that Carina--(reference, evidently, to hostess, whose name is Charlotte Volley)–is Perfectly Wonderful. Her Work is Wonderful, and so are her Methods, her Personality, her Vitality and her Charm.

I say Yes, a great many times, and feel that I can quite understand why Carina has Miss P. to live with her. (Am only too certain that neither Felicity nor dear Rose would dream of presenting me to visitors in similar light, should occasion for doing so ever arise.)

Carina and herself, continues Miss P., have been friends for many years now. She has nursed Carina through illness--Carina is not at all strong--and never, never rests. If only she would sometimes *spare* herself, says Miss P. despairingly--but, no, she has to be Giving Out all the time. People make demands upon her. If it isn't one, it's another.

At this, I feel guilty, and suggest departure. Miss P. protests, but faintly, and is evidently in favour of scheme. Carina is approached, but says, No, no, we must stay to tea, we are expected. Miss P. murmurs energetically, and is told, No, no, *that* doesn't matter, and Felicity and I feign absorption in small and unpleasant-looking yellow plant at our feet. Later, Miss P. admits to me that Carina ought to relax *absolutely* for at least an hour every afternoon, but that it is terribly, terribly difficult to get her to do it. To-day's failure evidently lies at our door, and Miss P. remains dejected, and faintly resentful, until we finally depart.

Carina is cordial to the last, sees us into car, has to be told that *that* door won't open, will she try the other side, does so, shuts it briskly, and says that we must come again *soon*. Final view of her is with her arm round Miss P.'s shoulder, waving vigorously. What, I immediately enquire, did Felicity think of her? to which Felicity replies with some bitterness that it is not a very good moment for her to give an opinion, as Carina has just energetically slammed door of the car upon her foot.

Condolences follow, and we discuss Carina, Miss P., cousin, house, garden, food and conversation, all the way home. Should be quite prepared to do so all over again for benefit of Robert in the evening, but he shows no interest, after enquiring whether there wasn't a man anywhere about the place, and being told Only the Gardener.

April 23rd.–Felicity and I fetch as many of Carina's works as we can collect from Boots', and read them industriously. Great excitement on discovering that one of them--the best known--is dedicated to Carina's Beloved Friend, D. P., whom we immediately identify as Miss Postman, Felicity maintaining that D. stands for Daisy, whilst I hold out for Doris. Discussion closes with ribald reference to *Well of Loneliness.*

April 26th.–Felicity, after altering her mind three times, departs, to stay with married sister in Somersetshire. Robin and Vicky lament and I say that we shall all miss her, and she replies that she has loved being here, and it is the only house she knows where the bath towels are really *large*. Am gratified by this compliment, and subsequently repeat it to Robert, adding that it proves I *can't* be such a bad housekeeper. Robert looks indulgent, but asks what about that time we ran out of flour just before a Bank Holiday week-end? To which I make no reply--being unable to think of a good one.

Telephone message from Lady Frobisher, inviting us to dinner on Saturday next, as the dear Blamingtons will be with her for the weekend. I say The Blamingtons? in enquiring tones, and she says Yes, yes, *he* knew me very well indeed eighteen years ago, and admired me tremendously. (This seems to me to constitute excellent reason why we should not meet again, merely in order to be confronted with deplorable alterations wrought by the passage of eighteen years.)

Lady F., however, says that she has promised to produce me--and Robert, too, of course, she adds hastily--and we *must* come. The Blaming-tons are wildly excited. (Have idle and frivolous vision of the Blamingtons standing screaming and dancing at her elbow, waiting to hear decision.)

But, says Lady F., in *those* days--reference as to period preceding the Stone Age at least--in *those* days, I probably knew him as Bill Ransom? He has only this moment come into the title. I say Oh! *Bill Ransom*, and lapse into shattered silence, while Lady F. goes on to tell me what an extraordinarily pretty, intelligent, attractive and wealthy woman Bill has married, and how successful the marriage is. (Am by no means disposed to credit this offhand.)

Conversation closes with renewed assurances from Lady F. of the Blamingtons' and her own cast-iron determination that they shall not leave the neighbourhood without scene of reunion between Bill and myself, and my own enfeebled assent to this preposterous scheme.

Spend at least ten minutes sitting by the telephone, still grasping receiver, wondering what Bill and I are going to think of one another, when compelled to meet, and why on earth I ever agreed to anything so senseless.

Tell Robert about invitation, and he says Good, the Frobishers have excellent claret, but remains totally unmoved at prospect of the Blamingtons. This--perhaps unjustly--annoys me, and I answer sharply that Bill Ransom once liked me very much indeed, to which Robert absently replies that he daresays, and turns on the wireless. I raise my voice, in order to dominate Happy Returns to Patricia Trabbs of Streatham, and screech that Bill several times asked me to marry him, and Robert nods, and walks out through the window into the garden.

Helen Wills and children rush in at the door, draught causes large vase to blow over, and inundate entire room with floods of water, and incredibly numerous fragments of ribes-flower, and all is merged into frantic moppings and sweepings, and adjurations to children not to cut themselves with broken glass. Happy Families follows, immediately succeeded by Vicky's bath, and supper for both, and far-distant indiscretions of self and Bill Ransom return to oblivion, but recrudesce much later, when children have gone to bed, Casabianca is muttering quietly to himself over cross-word puzzle, and Robert absorbed in *Times*.

Take up a book and read several pages, but presently discover that I have no idea what it is all about, and begin all over again, with similar result. Casabianca suddenly remarks that he would so much like to know what I think of that book, to which I hastily reply Oh! very good indeed, and he says he thought so too, and I offer help with cross-word puzzle in order to stem further discussion.

Spend much time in arranging how I can best get in to hairdresser's for shampoo-and-set before Saturday, and also consider purchase of new frock, but am aware that financial situation offers no justification whatever for this.

Much later on, Robert enquires whether I am ill, and on receiving negative reply, urges that I should try and get to sleep. As I have been doing this, without success, for some time, answer appears to me to be unnecessary.

(*Mem.:* Self-control very, very desirable quality, especially where imagination involved, and must certainly endeavour to cultivate.)

April 30th.–Incredible quantity of household requirements immediately springs into life on my announcing intention of going into Plymouth in order to visit hairdresser. Even Casabianca suddenly says Would it be troubling me too much to ask me to get a postal-order for three shillings and tenpence-halfpenny? Reply tartly that he will find an equally acceptable one at village Post Office, and then wish I hadn't when he meekly begs my pardon and says that, Yes, of course he can.

(*N.B.* This turning of the cheek has effect, as usual, of making me much crosser than before. Feel that doubt is being cast on Scriptural advice, and dismiss subject immediately.)

Bus takes me to Plymouth, where I struggle with Haberdashery--wholly uncongenial form of shopping, and extraordinarily exhausting--socks for Vicky, pants for Robin, short scrubbing-brush demanded by Cook, but cannot imagine what she means to do with it, or why it has to be short--also colossal list of obscure groceries declared to be unobtainable anywhere nearer than Plymouth. None of these are ever in stock at counters where I ask for them, and have to be procured either Upstairs or in the Basement, and am reminded of comic song prevalent in days of youth: The Other Department, If you please, Straight On and Up the Stairs. Quote it to grey-headed shopman, in whom I think it may rouse memories, but he only replies Just so, moddam, and we part without further advances on either side.

Rather tedious encounter follows with young gentleman presiding over Pickles, who endeavours to persuade me that I want particularly expensive brand of chutney instead of that which I have asked for, and which he cannot supply. Am well aware that I ought to cut him short with curt assurance that No Substitute will Do, but find myself mysteriously unable to do anything of the kind, and we continue to argue round and round in a circle, although without acrimony on either side. Curious and unsatisfactory conclusion is reached by my abandoning Chutney *motif* altogether, and buying small and unknown brand of cheese in a little jar. Young gentleman then becomes conversational in lighter vein, and tells me of his preference in films, and we agree that No-one has ever come near Dear Old Charlie. Nor ever will, says the young gentleman conclusively, as he ties string into elegant bow, which will give way the moment I get into street. I say No indeed, we exchange mutual expressions of gratitude, and I perceive that I am going to be late for appointment with hairdresser.

Collect number of small parcels--including particularly degraded-looking paper-bag containing Chips for which Robin and Vicky have implored--sling them from every available finger until I look like inferior Christmas-tree, thrust library-books under one arm--(they slip continually, and have to be pushed into safety from behind by means of ungraceful acrobatics)--and emerge into street. Unendearing glimpse of myself as I pass looking-glass reveals that my hat has apparently engulfed the whole of my head and half of my face as well. (Disquieting query here: Is this perhaps all for the best?) Also that blue coat with fur collar, reasonably becoming when I left home, has now assumed aspect of something out of a second-hand clothes-shop. Encourage myself with visions of unsurpassed brilliance that is to be mine after shampoo-and-set, careful dressing to-night, and liberal application of face-powder, and--if necessary--rouge.

Just as I have, mentally, seen exquisite Paris-model gown that exactly fits me, for sale in draper's window at improbable price of forty-nine shillings and sixpence, am recalled to reality by loud and cordial greetings of Our Vicar's Wife, who plunges through traffic at great risk to life in order to say what a coincidence this is, considering that we met yesterday, and are sure to be meeting to-morrow. She also invites me to come and help her choose white linen buttons for pillow-cases--but this evidently leading direct to Haberdashery once more, and I refuse--I hope with convincing appearance of regret.

Am subsequently dealt with by hairdresser--who says that I am the only lady he knows that still wears a bob--and once more achieve bus, where I meet Miss S. of the Post Office, who has also been shopping. We agree that a day's shopping is tiring--One's Feet, says Miss S.--and that the bus hours are inconvenient. Still, we can't hope for everything in this world, and Miss S. admits that she is looking forward to a Nice Cup of Tea and perhaps a Lay-Down, when she gets home. Reflect, not for the first time, that there are advantages in being a spinster. Should be sorry to say exactly how long it is since I last had a Lay-Down myself, without being disturbed at least fourteen times in the course of it.

Spend much time, on reaching home, in unpacking and distributing household requirements, folding up and putting away paper and string, and condoling with Vicky, who alleges that Casabianca had made her walk miles and *miles*, and she has a pain in her wrist. Do not attempt to connect these two statements, but suggest the sofa and *Dr. Dolittle*, to which Vicky agrees with air of exhaustion, which is greatly intensified every time she catches my eye.

Later on, Casabianca turns up--looking pale-green with cold and making straight for the fire--and announces that he and the children have had a Splendid Walk and are all the better for it. Since I know, and Vicky knows, that this is being said for the express benefit of Vicky, we receive it rather tepidly, and conversation lapses while I pursue elusive sum of ten shillings and threepence through shopping accounts. Robin comes in by the window--I say, too late, Oh, your *boots*!–and Robert, unfortunately choosing this moment to appear, enquires whether there isn't a schoolroom in the house?

Atmosphere by this time is quite unfavourable to festivity, and I go up to dress for the Frobishers--or, more accurately, for the Blamingtons--feeling limp.

Hot bath restores me slightly--but relapse occurs when entirely vital shoulder-strap gives way and needle and thread become necessary.

Put on my Green, dislike it very much indeed, and once more survey contents of wardrobe, as though expecting to find miraculous addition to already perfectly well-known contents.

Needless to say, this does not happen, and after some contemplation of my Black--which looks rusty and entirely out of date--and my Blue--which is a candidate for the next Jumble sale--I return to the looking-glass still in my Green, and gaze at myself earnestly.

(*Query:* Does this denote irrational hope of sudden and complete transformation in personal appearance? If so, can only wonder that so much faith should meet with so little reward.)

Jewel-case unfortunately rather low at present--(have every hope of restoring at least part of the contents next month, if American sales satisfactory)–but great-aunt's diamond ring fortunately still with us, and I put it on fourth finger of left hand, and hope that Bill will think Robert gave it to me. Exact motive governing this wish far too complicated to be analysed, but shelve entire question by saying to myself that Anyway, Robert certainly *would* have given it to me if he could have afforded it.

Evening cloak is smarter than musquash coat; put it on. Robert says Am I off my head and do I want to arrive frozen? Brief discussion follows, but I know he is right and I am wrong, and eventually compromise by putting on fur coat, and carrying cloak, to make decent appearance with on arrival in hall.

Fausse sortie ensues--as it so frequently does in domestic surroundings--and am twice recalled on the very verge of departure, once by Ethel, with superfluous observation that she supposes she had better not lock up at ten o'clock, and once by Robin, who takes me aside and says that he is very sorry, he has broken his bedroom window. It was, he says, entirely an accident, as he was only kicking his football about. I point out briefly, but kindly, that accidents of this nature are avoidable, and we part affectionately. Robert, at the wheel, looks patient, and I feel perfectly convinced that entire evening is going to be a failure.

Nobody in drawing-room when we arrive, and butler looks disapprovingly round, as though afraid that Lady F. or Sir William may be quietly hiding under some of the furniture, but this proving groundless, he says that he will Inform Her Ladyship, and leaves us. I immediately look in the glass, which turns out to be an ancient Italian treasure, and shows me a pale yellow reflection, with one eye much higher than the other. Before I have in any way recovered, Lady F. is in the room, so is Sir William, and so are the Blamingtons. Have not the slightest idea what happens next, but can see that Bill, except that he has grown bald, is unaltered, and has kept his figure, and that I do not like the look of his wife, who has lovely hair, a Paris frock, and is elaborately made-up.

We all talk a great deal about the weather, which is--as usual--cold, and I hear myself assuring Sir W. that our rhododendrons are not yet showing a single bud. Sir W. expresses astonishment--which would be even greater if he realised that we only have one rhododendron in the world, and that I haven't set eyes on it for weeks owing to pressure of indoor occupations--and we go in to dinner. I am placed between Sir W. and Bill, and Bill looks at me and says Well, well, and we talk about Hampstead, and mutual friends, of whom Bill says Do you ever see anything of them nowadays? to which I am invariably obliged to reply No, we haven't met for years. Bill makes the best of this by observing civilly that I am lucky to live in such a lovely part of the world, and he supposes we have a very charming house, to which I reply captiously No, quite ordinary, and we both laugh.

Conversation after this much easier, and I learn that Bill has two children, a boy and a girl. I say that I have the same, and, before I can stop myself, have added that this is really a most extraordinary coincidence. Wish I hadn't been so emphatic about it, and hastily begin to talk about aviation to Sir William. He has a great deal to say about this, and I ejaculate Yes at intervals, and ascertain that Bill's wife is telling Robert that the policy of the Labour party is suicidal, to which he assents heartily, and that Lady F. and Bill are exchanging views about Norway.

Shortly after this, conversation becomes general, party-politics predominating--everyone except myself apparently holding Conservative views, and taking it for granted that none other exist in civilised circles--and I lapse into silence.

(*Query:* Would not a greater degree of moral courage lead me to straightforward and open declaration of precise attitude held by myself in regard to the Conservative and other parties? *Answer:* Indubitably, yes--but results of such candour not improbably disastrous, and would assuredly add little to social amenities of present occasion.)

Entirely admirable dinner brought to a close with South African pears, and Lady F. says Shall we have coffee in the drawing-room?–entirely rhetorical question, as decision naturally rests with herself.

Customary quarter of an hour follows, during which I look at Bill's wife, and like her less than ever, especially when she and Lady F. discuss hairdressers, and topic of Permanent Waves being introduced--(probably on purpose)-by Bill's wife, she says that her own is Perfectly Natural, which I feel certain, to my disgust, is the truth.

It transpires that she knows Pamela Pringle, and later on she tells Bill that Pamela P. is a great friend of mine, and adds Fancy! which I consider offensive, *whatever* it means.

Bridge follows--I play with Sir William, and do well, but as Robert loses heavily, exchequer will not materially benefit--and evening draws to a close.

Hold short conversation with Bill in the hall whilst Robert is getting the car. He says that Sevenoaks is all on our way to London whenever we motor up--which we never do, and it wouldn't be even if we did--and it would be very nice if we'd stay a night or two. I say Yes, we'd love that, and we agree that It's a Promise, and both know very well that it isn't, and Robert reappears and everybody says good-bye.

Experience extraordinary medley of sensations as we drive away, and journey is accomplished practically in silence.

May 1st.–I ask Robert if he thought Lady Blamington good-looking, and he replies that he wouldn't say *that* exactly. What would he say, then? Well, he would say striking, perhaps. He adds that he'll eat his hat if they have a penny less than twenty-thousand a year between them, and old Frobisher says that their place in Kent is a show place. I ask what he thought of Bill, and Robert says Oh, he seemed all right. Make final enquiry as to what *I* looked like last night, and whether Robert thinks that eighteen years makes much difference in one's appearance?

Robert, perhaps rightly, ignores the last half of this, and replies to the former--after some thought--that I looked just as usual, but he doesn't care much about that green dress. Am sufficiently unwise to press for further information, at which Robert looks worried, but finally admits that, to his mind, the green dress makes me look Tawdry.

Am completely disintegrated by this adjective, which recurs to me in the midst of whatever I am doing, for the whole of the remainder of the day.

Activities mainly concerned with school-clothes, of which vast quantities are required by both children, Robin owing to school exigencies, and Vicky to inordinately rapid growth. Effect on domestic finances utterly disastrous in either case. Robin's trunk is brought down from the attic, and Vicky's suitcase extracted from beneath bed. Casabianca and the gardener are obliged to deal with Casabianca's trunk, which is of immense size and weight, and sticks on attic staircase.

(*Query, of entirely private nature:* Why cannot Casabianca travel about with reasonable luggage like anybody else? Is he concealing murdered body or other incriminating evidence from which he dares not be parted? *Answer:* Can obviously never be known.)

Second post brings unexpected and most surprising letter from Mademoiselle, announcing that she is in England and cannot wait to embrace us once again--may she have one sight of Vicky--*ce petit ange*–and Robin--*ce gentil gosse*–before they return to school? She will willingly, in order to obtain this privilege, *courir nu-pieds* from Essex to Devonshire. Despatch immediate telegram inviting her for two nights, and debate desirability of adding that proposed barefooted Marathon wholly unnecessary--but difficulty of including this in twelve words deters me, moreover French sense of humour always incalculable to a degree. Announce impending visit to children, who receive it much as I expected. Robin says Oh, and continues to decipher "John Brown's Body" very slowly on the piano with one finger--which he has done almost hourly every day these holidays--and Vicky looks blank and eats unholy-looking mauve lozenge alleged to be a present from Cook.

(*Mem.*: Speak to Cook, tactfully and at the same time decisively. Must think this well out beforehand.)

Robert's reaction to approaching union with devoted friend and guardian of Vicky's infancy lacking in any enthusiasm whatever.

May 3rd.–Mademoiselle arrives by earlier train than was expected, and is deposited at front door, in the middle of lunch, by taxi, together with rattan basket, secured by cord, small attaché case, large leather hat-box, plaid travelling rug, parcel wrapped in American oilcloth, and two hand-bags.

We all rush out (excepting Helen Wills, who is subsequently found to have eaten the butter off dish on sideboard) and much excitement follows. If Mademoiselle says *Ah, mais ce qu'ils ont grandis!* once, she says it thirty-five times. To me she exclaims that I have *bonne mine*, and do not look a day over twenty, which is manifestly absurd. Robert shakes hands with her--at which she cries *Ah! quelle bonne poignée de main anglaise!* and introduction of Casabianca is effected, but this less successful, and rather distant bows are exchanged, and I suggest adjournment to din in groom.

Lunch resumed--roast lamb and mint sauce recalled for Mademoiselle's benefit, and am relieved at respectable appearance they still present, which could never have been the case with either cottage pie or Irish stew--and news is exchanged. Mademoiselle has, it appears, accepted another post--doctor's household in *les environs de Londres*, which I think means Putney--but has touchingly stipulated for two days in which to visit us before embarking on new duties.

I say how glad I am, and she says, once more, that the children have grown, and throws up both hands towards the ceiling and tosses her head.

Suggestion, from Robert, that Robin and Vicky should take their oranges into the garden, is adopted, and Casabianca escorts them from the room.

Mademoiselle immediately enquires *Qu'est-ce que c'est que ce petit jeune homme?* in tones perfectly, and I think designedly, audible from the hall where Vicky and Casabianca can be heard in brisk dispute over a question of goloshes. I reply, in rebukefully lowered voice, with short outline of Casabianca's position in household--which is, to my certain knowledge, perfectly well known to Mademoiselle already. She slightingly replies *Tiens, c'est drôle*–words and intonation both, in my opinion, entirely unnecessary. The whole of this dialogue rouses in me grave apprehension as to success or otherwise of next forty-eight hours.

Mademoiselle goes to unpack, escorted by Vicky--should like to think this move wholly inspired by grateful affection, but am more than doubtful--Casabianca walks Robin up and down the lawn, obviously for purpose of admonishment--probably justifiable, but faint feeling of indignation assails me at the sight--and I stand idle just outside hall-door until Robert goes past me with a wheelbarrow and looks astonished, when I remember that I must (a) Write letters, (b) Telephone to the Bread, which ought to be here and isn't, (c) Go on sorting school clothes, (d) Put Cash's initials on Vicky's new stockings, (e) See about sending nursery chintzes to the cleaners.

Curious and unprofitable reflection crosses my mind that if I were the heroine of a novel, recent encounter between Bill and myself would lead to further developments of tense and emotional description, culminating either in renunciation, or--if novel a modern one--complete flight of cap over windmill.

Real life, as usual, totally removed from literary conventions, and nothing remains but to hasten indoors and deal with accumulated household duties.

Arrival of second post, later on, gives rise to faint recrudescence of romantic speculations, when letter in unknown, but educated, handwriting, bearing London postmark, is handed to me. Have mentally taken journey to Paris, met Bill by appointment, and said good-bye to him for ever--and also, alternatively, gone with him to the South Sea Islands, been divorced by Robert, and heard of the deaths of both children--before opening letter. It turns out to be from unknown gentleman of high military rank, who asks me whether I am interested in the New Economy, as he is selling off mild-cured hams very cheaply indeed.

May 5th.–Fears relating to perfect harmony between Mademoiselle and Casabianca appear to have been well founded, and am relieved that entire party disperses to-morrow. Children, as usual on last day of holidays, extremely exuberant, but am aware, from previous experience, that fearful reaction will set in at eleventh hour.

Decide on picnic, said to be in Mademoiselle's honour, and Robert tells me privately that he thinks Casabianca had better be left behind. Am entirely of opinion that he is right, and spend some time in evolving graceful and kindhearted little formula with which to announce this arrangement, but all ends in failure.

Casabianca says Oh no, it is very kind of me, but he would quite enjoy a picnic, and does not want an afternoon to himself. He has no letters to write--very kind of me to think of such a thing. Nor does he care about a quiet day in the garden, kind though it is of me. Final desperate suggestion that he would perhaps appreciate vague and general asset of A Free Day, he receives with renewed reference to my extreme kindness, and incontrovertible statement that he wouldn't know what to do with a free day if he had it.

Retire defeated, and tell Robert that Casabianca *wants* to come to the picnic--which Robert appears to think unnatural in the extreme. Towards three o'clock it leaves off raining, and we start, customary collection of rugs, mackintoshes, baskets and thermos flasks in back of car.

Mademoiselle says *Ah, combien ça me rappelle le passé que nous ne reverrons plus!* and rolls her eyes in the direction of Casabianca, and I remember with some thankfulness that his knowledge of French is definitely limited. Something tells me, however, that he has correctly interpreted meaning of Mademoiselle's glance.

Rain begins again, and by the time we reach appointed beauty-spot is falling very briskly indeed. Robert, who has left home under strong compulsion from Vicky, is now determined to see the thing through, and announces that he shall walk the dog to the top of the hill, and that the children had better come too. Mademoiselle, shrouded in large plaid cape, exerts herself in quite unprecedented manner, and offers to go with them, which shames me into doing likewise, sorely against my inclination. We all get very wet indeed, and Vicky falls into mysterious gap in a hedge and comes out dripping and with black smears that turn out to be tar all over her.

Mon Dieu, says Mademoiselle, *il n'y a donc plus personne pour s'occuper de cette malheureuse petite?* Should like to remind her of many, many similar misfortunes which have befallen Vicky under Mademoiselle's own supervision--but do not, naturally, do so.

TENSION AT THE PICNIC

Situation, already slightly tense, greatly aggravated by Casabianca, who selects this ill-judged moment for rebuking Vicky at great length, at which Mademoiselle exclaims passionately *Ah ma bonne Sainte Vierge, ayez pitié de nous!* which strikes us all into a deathly silence.

Rain comes down in torrents, and I suggest tea in the car, but this is abandoned when it becomes evident that we are too tightly packed to be able to open baskets, let alone spread out their contents. Why not tea in the dining-room at home? is Robert's contribution towards solving difficulty, backed quietly, but persistently, by Casabianca. This has immediate effect of causing Mademoiselle to advocate *un goûter en plein air*, as though we were at Fontainebleau, or any other improbable spot, in blazing sunshine.

Robin suddenly and brilliantly announces that we are quite near Bull Alley Manor, which is empty, and that the gardener will allow us to have a picnic in the hen-house. Everybody says The Hen-house? except Vicky, who screams and looks enchanted, and Mademoiselle, who also screams, and refers to *punaises*, which she declares will abound. Robin explains that he means a summer-house on the Bull Alley tennis-ground, which has a wire-netting and *looks* like a hen-house, but he doesn't think it really is. He adds triumphantly that it has a bench that we can sit on. Robert puts in a final plea for the dining-room at home, but without conviction, and we drive ten miles to Bull Alley Manor, where picnic takes place under Robin's auspices, all of us sitting in a row on long wooden seat, exactly like old-fashioned school feast. I say that it reminds me of *The Daisy Chain*, but nobody knows what I mean, and reference is allowed to drop while we eat potted-meat sandwiches and drink lemonade, which is full of pips.

Return home at half-past six, feeling extraordinarily exhausted. Find letter from Literary Agent, suggesting that the moment has now come when fresh masterpiece from my pen may definitely be expected, and may he hope to receive my new manuscript quite shortly? Idle fancy, probably born of extreme fatigue, crosses my mind as to results of a perfectly candid reply--to the effect that literary projects entirely swamped by hourly activities concerned with children, housekeeping, sewing, letter-writing, Women's Institute Meetings, and absolute necessity of getting eight hours' sleep every night.

Decide that another visit to Doughty Street is imperative, and say to Robert, feebly and untruthfully, that I am sure he would not mind my spending a week or two in London, to get some writing done. To this Mademoiselle, officiously and unnecessarily, adds that, naturally, *madame désire se distraire de temps en temps*–which is not in the least what I want to convey.

Robert says nothing, but raises one eyebrow.

May 6th.–Customary heart-rending half-hour in which Robin and Vicky appear to realise for the first time since last holidays that they must return to school. Robin says nothing whatever, but turns gradually *eau-de-nil*, and Vicky proclaims that she feels almost certain she will not be able to survive the first night away from home. I tell myself firmly that, as a modern mother, I must be Bracing, but very inconvenient lump in my throat renders this difficult, and I suggest instead that they should go and say good-bye to the gardener.

Luggage, which has theoretically been kept within very decent limits, fills the hall and overflows outside front door, and Casabianca's trunk threatens to take entire car all to itself. Mademoiselle eyes it disparagingly and says *Ciel! on dirait tout un déménagement*, but relents at the moment of farewell, and gives Casabianca her hand remarking *Sans rancune, hein?* which he fortunately does not understand, and can therefore not reply to, except by rather chilly bow, elegantly executed from the waist. Mademoiselle then without warning bursts into tears, kisses children and myself, says *On se reverra au Paradis, au moins*–which is on the whole optimistic--and is driven by Robert to the station.

Hired car removes Casabianca, after customary exchange of compliments between us, and extraordinarily candid display of utter indifference from both Robin and Vicky, and I take them to the Junction, when unknown parent of unknown schoolfellow of Robin's takes charge of him with six other boys, who all look to me exactly alike.

Vicky weeps, and I give her an ice and then escort her to station all over again, and put her in charge of the guard to whom she immediately says Can she go in the Van with him? He agrees, and they disappear hand-in-hand.

Drive home again, and avoid the nursery for the rest of the day. *May 10th.*–Decide that a return to Doughty Street flat is imperative, and try to make clear to Robert that this course really represents Economy in the Long Run. Mentally assemble superb array of evidence to this effect, but it unfortunately eludes me when trying to put it into words and all becomes feeble and incoherent. Also observe in myself tendency to repeat over and over again rather unmeaning formula: It Isn't as if It was going to be For Long, although perfectly well aware that Robert heard me the first time, and was unimpressed. Discussion closes with my fetching A.B.C. out of the dining-room, and discovering that it dates from 1929.

May 17th.–Return to Doughty Street flat, and experience immense and unreasonable astonishment at finding it almost exactly as I left it, yellow-and-white check dust-sheets and all. Am completely entranced, and spend entire afternoon and evening arranging two vases of flowers, unpacking suit-case and buying tea and biscuits in Gray's Inn Road where I narrowly escape extinction under a tram.

Perceive that Everybody in the World except myself is wearing long skirts, a tiny hat on extreme back of head, and vermilion lip-stick. Look at myself in the glass and resolve instantly to visit Hairdresser, Beauty Parlour, and section of large Store entitled Inexpensive Small Ladies, before doing anything else at all.

Ring up Rose, who says Oh, am I back?–which I obviously must be--and charmingly suggests dinner next week--two friends whom she wants me to meet--and a luncheon party at which I must come and help her. Am flattered, and say Yes, yes, how? to which Rose strangely replies, By leaving rather early, if I don't mind, as this may break up the party.

Note: Extraordinary revelations undoubtedly hidden below much so-called hospitality, if inner thoughts of many hostesses were to be revealed. This thought remains persistently with me, in spite of explanation from Rose that she has appointment miles away at three o'clock, on day of luncheon, and is afraid of not getting there punctually. Agree, but without enthusiasm, to leave at half-past two in the hopes of inducing fellow-guests to do likewise.

Rose also enquires, with some unnecessary mirth, whether I am going to Do Anything about my little friend Pamela Pringle, to which I reply Not that I know of, and say Good-night and ring off. Completely incredible coincidence ensues, and am rung up five minutes later by P. P. who alleges that she "had a feeling" I should be in London again. Become utterly helpless in the face of this prescience, and agree in enthusiastic terms to come to a cocktail party at Pamela's flat, meet her for a long talk at her Club, and go with her to the Royal Academy one morning. Entire prospect fills me with utter dismay, and go to bed in completely dazed condition.

Pamela rings up again just before midnight, and hopes so, so much she hasn't disturbed me or anything like that, but she forgot to say--she knows so well that I shan't misunderstand--there's nothing in it at all--only if a letter comes for her addressed to my flat, will I just keep it till we meet? Quite likely it won't come at all, but *if* it does, will I just do that and not say anything about it, as people are so terribly apt to misunderstand the simplest thing? Am I sure I don't mind? As by this time I mind nothing at all except being kept out of my bed any longer, I agree to everything, say that I understand absolutely, and am effusively thanked by Pamela and rung off.

May 21st.–Attend Pamela Pringle's cocktail party after much heart-searching as to suitable clothes for the occasion. Consult Felicity--on a postcard--who replies--on a postcard--that she hasn't the least idea, also Emma Hay (this solely because I happen to meet her in King's Road, Chelsea, not because I have remotest intention of taking her advice). Emma says lightly Oh, pyjamas are the thing, she supposes, and I look at her and am filled with horror at implied suggestion that she herself ever appears anywhere in anything of the kind. But, says Emma, waving aside question which she evidently considers insignificant, Will I come with her next week to really delightful evening party in Bloomsbury, where every single Worth While Person in London is to be assembled? Suggest in reply, with humorous intention, that the British Museum has, no doubt, been reserved to accommodate them all, but Emma not in the least amused, and merely replies No, a basement flat in Little James Street, if I know where that is. As it is within two minutes' walk of my own door, I do, and agree to be picked up by Emma and go on with her to the party.

She tells me that all London is talking about her slashing attack on G. B. Stern's new novel, and what did I feel? I ask where the slashing attack is to be found, and Emma exclaims Do I really mean that I haven't seen this month's *Hampstead Clarionet?* and I reply with great presence of mind but total disregard for truth, that they've probably Sold Out, at which Emma, though obviously astounded, agrees that that must be it, and we part amiably.

Question of clothes remains unsolved until eleventh hour, when I decide on black crêpe-de-chine and new hat that I think becoming.

Bus No. 19, as usual, takes me to Sloane Street, and I reach flat door at half-past six, and am taken up in lift, hall-porter--one of many--informing me on the way that I am the First. At this I beg to be taken down again and allowed to wait in the hall, but he replies, not unreasonably, that *Someone* has got to be first, miss. Revive at being called miss, and allow myself to be put down in front of P. P.'s door, where porter rings the bell as if he didn't altogether trust me to do it for myself--in which he is right--and I subsequently crawl, rather than walk, into Pamela's drawing-room. Severe shock ensues when Pamela--wearing pale pink flowered chiffon--reveals herself in perfectly bran-new incarnation as purest platinum blonde. Recover from this with what I consider well-bred presence of mind, but am shattered anew by passionate enquiry from Pamela as to whether I like it. Reply, quite truthfully, that she looks lovely, and all is harmony. I apologise for arriving early, and Pamela assures me that she is only too glad, and adds that she wouldn't have been here herself as early as this if her bedroom clock hadn't been an hour fast, and she wants to hear all my news. She then tells me all hers, which is mainly concerned with utterly unaccountable attitude of Waddell, who goes into a fit if any man under ninety so much as *looks* at Pamela. (Am appalled at cataclysmic nature of Waddell's entire existence, if this is indeed the case.)

Previous experience of Pamela's parties leads me to enquire if Waddell is to be present this afternoon, at which she looks astonished and says Oh Yes, she supposes so, he is quite a good host in his own way, and anyway she is sure he would adore to see me.

(Waddell and I have met exactly once before, on which occasion we did not speak, and am morally certain that he would not know me again if he saw me.)

Bell rings, and influx of very young gentlemen supervenes, and are all greeted by Pamela and introduced to me as Tim and Nicky and the Twins. I remain anonymous throughout, but Pamela lavishly announces that I am very, very clever and literary--with customary result of sending all the very young gentlemen into the furthermost corner of the room, from whence they occasionally look over their shoulders at me with expressions of acute horror.

They are followed by Waddell--escorting, to my immense relief, Rose's Viscountess, whom I greet as an old friend, at which she seems faintly surprised, although in quite a kind way--and elderly American with a bald head. He sits next me, and wants to know about Flag-days, and--after drinking something out of a little glass handed me in a detached way by one of the very young gentlemen--I suddenly find myself extraordinarily eloquent and informative on the subject.

Elderly American encourages me by looking at me thoughtfully and attentively while I speak--(difference in this respect between Americans and ourselves is marked, and greatly to the advantage of the former)--and saying at intervals that what I am telling him Means Quite a Lot to him--which is more than it does to me. Long before I think I have exhausted the subject, Pamela removes the American by perfectly simple and direct method of telling him to come and talk to her, which he obediently does--but bows at me rather apologetically first.

THE POLITE AMERICAN

Waddell immediately refills my glass, although without speaking a word, and Rose's Viscountess talks to me about *Time and Tide*. We spend a pleasant five minutes, and at the end of them I have promised to go and see her, and we have exchanged Christian names. Can this goodwill be due to alcohol? Have a dim idea that this question had better not be propounded at the moment.

Room is by this time entirely filled with men, cigarette smoke and conversation. Have twice said No, really, not any more thank you, to Waddell, and he has twice ignored it altogether, and continued to pour things into my glass, and I to drink them. Result is a very strange mixture of exhilaration, utter recklessness and rather sentimental melancholy. Am also definitely feeling giddy and aware that this will be much worse as soon as I attempt to stand up.

Unknown man, very attractive, sitting near me, tells me of very singular misfortune that has that day befallen him. He has, to his infinite distress, dealt severe blow with a walking-stick to strange woman, totally unknown to him, outside the Athenaeum. I say Really, in concerned tones, Was that just an accident? Oh, yes, purest accident. He was showing a friend how to play a stroke at golf, and failed to perceive woman immediately behind him. This unhappily resulted in the breaking of her spectacles, and gathering of a large crowd, and moral obligation on his own part to drive her immense distance in a taxi to see (a) a doctor, (b) an oculist,(c) her husband, who turns out to live at Richmond. I sympathise passionately, and suggest that he will probably have to keep both woman and her husband for the rest of their lives, which, he says, had already occurred to him.

This dismays us both almost equally, and we each drink another cocktail.

Pamela--had already wondered why she had left attractive unknown to me so long--now breaks up this agreeable conversation, by saying that Waddell will never, never, forgive anybody else for monopolising me, and I simply must do my best to put him into a really *good* mood, as Pamela has got to tell him about her dressmaker's bill presently, so will I be an angel--? She then removes delightful stranger, and I am left in a dazed condition. Have dim idea that Waddell is reluctantly compelled by Pamela to join me, and that we repeatedly assure one another that there are No Good Plays Running Nowadays. Effect of this eclectic pronouncement rather neutralised later, when it turns out that Waddell never patronises anything except talkies, and that I haven't set foot inside a London theatre for eight-and-a-half months.

Later still it dawns on me that I am almost the last person left at the party, except for Waddell, who has turned on the wireless and is listening to Vaudeville, and Pamela, who is on the sofa having her palm read by one young man, while two others hang over the back of it and listen attentively.

I murmur a very general and unobtrusive good-bye, and go away. Am not certain, but think that hall-porter eyes me compassionately, but we content ourselves with exchange of rather grave smiles--no words.

Am obliged to return to Doughty Street in a taxi, owing to very serious fear that I no longer have perfect control over my legs.

Go instantly to bed on reaching flat, and room whirls round and round in distressing fashion for some time before I go to sleep.

May 25th.–Life one round of gaiety, and feel extremely guilty on receiving a letter from Our Vicar's Wife, saying that she is certain I am working hard at a New Book, and she should so like to hear what it's all about and what its name is. If I will tell her this, she will speak to the girl at Boots', as every little helps. She herself is extremely busy, and the garden is looking nice, but everything very late this year. P.S. Have I heard that old Mrs. Blenkinsopp is going to Bournemouth?

Make up my mind to write really long and interesting reply to this, but when I sit down to do so find that I am quite unable to write anything at all, except items that would appear either indiscreet, boastful or scandalous. Decide to wait until after Emma Hay's party in Little James Street, as this will give me something to write about.

(*Mem.:* Self-deception almost certainly involved here, as reflection makes it perfectly evident that Our Vicar's Wife is unlikely in the extreme to be either amused or edified by the antics of any acquaintances brought to my notice via Emma.)

Go down to Mickleham by bus--which takes an hour and a half--to see Vicky, who is very lively and affectionate, and looks particularly well, but declares herself to be overworked. I ask What at? and she says Oh, Eurhythmics. It subsequently appears that these take place one afternoon in every week, for one hour. She also says that she likes all her other lessons and is doing very well at them, and this is subsequently confirmed by higher authorities. Again patronise bus route--an hour and three-quarters, this time--and return to London, feeling exactly as if I had had a night journey to Scotland, travelling third-class and sitting bolt upright all the way.

May 26th.–Emma--in green sacque that looks exactly like *démodé* window-curtain, sandals and varnished toe-nails--calls for me at flat, and we go across to Little James Street. I ask whom I am going to meet and Emma replies, with customary spaciousness, Everyone, absolutely Everyone, but does not commit herself to names, or even numbers.

Exterior of Little James Street makes me wonder as to its capacities for dealing with Everyone, and this lack of confidence increases as Emma conducts me into extremely small house and down narrow flight of stone stairs, the whole culminating in long, thin room with black walls and yellow ceiling, apparently no furniture whatever, and curious, but no doubt interesting, collection of people all standing screaming at one another.

Emma looks delighted and says Didn't she tell me it would be a crush, that man over there is living with a negress now, and if she gets a chance she will bring him up to me.

(Should very much like to know with what object, since it will obviously be impossible for me to ask him the only thing I shall really be thinking about.)

Abstracted-looking man with a beard catches sight of Emma, and says Darling, in an absentminded manner, and then immediately moves away, followed, with some determination, by Emma.

Am struck by presence of many pairs of horn-rimmed spectacles, and marked absence of evening dress, also by very odd fact that almost everybody in the room has either abnormally straight or abnormally frizzy hair. Conversation in my vicinity is mainly concerned with astonishing picture on the wall, which I think represents Adam and Eve at very early stage indeed, but am by no means certain, and comments overheard do not enlighten me in the least. Am moreover seriously exercised in my mind as to exact meaning of *tempo, brio, appassionata* and *coloratura* as applied to art.

Strange man enters into conversation with me, but gives it up in disgust when I mention Adam and Eve, and am left with the impression--do not exactly know why--that picture in reality represents Sappho on the Isle of Lesbos.

(*Query:* Who was Sappho, and what was Isle of Lesbos?)

Emma presently reappears, leading reluctant-looking lady with red hair, and informs her in my presence that I am a country mouse--which infuriates me--and adds that we ought to get on well together, as we have identical inferiority complexes. Red-haired lady and I look at one another with mutual hatred, and separate as soon as possible, having merely exchanged brief comment on Adam and Eve picture, which she seems to think has something to do with the 'nineties and the *Yellow Book.*

Make one or two abortive efforts to find out if we have a host or hostess, and if so what they look like, and other more vigorous efforts to discover a chair, but all to no avail, and finally decide that as I am not enjoying myself, and am also becoming exhausted, I had better leave. Emma makes attempt that we both know to be half-hearted to dissuade me, and I rightly disregard it altogether, and prepare to walk out, Emma at the last moment shattering my nerve finally by asking what I think of that wonderful satirical study on the wall, epitomising the whole of the modern attitude towards Sex?

June 1st.–Life full of contrasts, as usual, and after recent orgy of Society, spend most of the day in washing white gloves and silk stockings, and drying them in front of electric fire. Effect of this on gloves not good, and remember too late that writer of Woman's Page in illustrated daily paper has always deprecated this practice.

Pay a call on Robert's Aunt Mary, who lives near Battersea Bridge, and we talk about relations. She says How do I think William and Angela are getting on? which sounds like preliminary to a scandal and excites me pleasurably, but it turns out to refer to recent venture in Beekeeping, no reference whatever to domestic situation, and William and Angela evidently giving no grounds for agitation at present.

Aunt Mary asks about children, says that school is a great mistake for girls, and that she does so hope Robin is good at games--which he isn't--and do I find that it answers to have A Man in the house? Misunderstanding occurs here, as I take this to mean Robert, but presently realise that it is Casabianca.

Tea and seed-cake appear, we partake, and Aunt Mary hopes that my writing does not interfere with home life and its many duties, and I hope so too, but in spite of this joint aspiration, impression prevails that we are mutually dissatisfied with one another. We part, and I go away feeling that I have been a failure. Wish I could believe that Aunt Mary was similarly downcast on her own account, but have noticed that this is seldom the case with older generation. Find extraordinary little envelope waiting for me at flat, containing printed assurance that I shall certainly be interested in recent curiosities of literature acquired by total stranger living in Northern manufacturing town, all or any of which he is prepared to send me under plain sealed cover. Details follow, and range from illustrated History of Flagellation to Unexpurgated Erotica.

Toy for some time with the idea that it is my duty to communicate with Scotland Yard, but officials there probably overworked already, and would be far more grateful for being left in peace, so take no action beyond consigning envelope and contents to the dust-bin.

June 9th.–Am rung up on the telephone by Editor of Time and Tide and told that We are Giving a Party on June 16th, at newest Park Lane Hotel. (Query: Is this the Editorial We, or does she conceivably mean she and I?–because if so, must at once disabuse her, owing to present financial state of affairs.) Will I serve on the Committee? Yes, I will. Who else is on it? Oh, says the Editor, Ellen Wilkinson is on it, only she won't be able to attend any of the meetings. I make civil pretence of thinking this a businesslike and helpful arrangement, and ask Who Else? Our Miss Lewis, says the Editor, and rings off before I can make further enquiries. Get into immediate touch with Our Miss Lewis, who turns out to be young, and full of activity. I make several suggestions, mostly to the effect that she should do a great deal of hard work, she accedes delightfully, and I am left with nothing to do except persuade highly distinguished Professor to take the Chair at Debate which is to be a feature of the party.

June 11th.–Distinguished Professor proves far less amenable than I had expected, and am obliged to call in Editorial assistance. Am informed by a side-wind that Distinguished Professor has said she Hates me, which seems to me neither dignified nor academic method of expressing herself--besides being definitely un-Christian.

Apart from this, preparations go on successfully, and I get myself a new frock for the occasion.

June 16th.–Reach Hotel at 4 o'clock, marvellous weather, frock very successful, and all is *couleur-de-rose.* Am met by official, to whom I murmur *Time and Tide*? and he commands minor official, at his elbow, to show Madam the Spanish Grill. (Extraordinary and unsuitable association at once springs to mind here, with Tortures of the Inquisition.) The Spanish Grill is surrounded by members of the *Time and Tide* Staff--Editor materialises, admirably dressed in black, and chills me to the heart by saying that as I happen to be here early I had better help her receive arrivals already beginning. (This does not strike me as a happy way of expressing herself.) Someone produces small label, bearing name by which I am--presumably--known to readers of *Time and Tide*, and this I pin to my frock, and feel exactly like one of the lesser exhibits at Madame Tussaud's.

Distinguished Professor, who does not greet me with any cordiality, is unnecessarily insistent on seeing that I do my duty, and places me firmly in receiving line. Several hundred millions then invade the Hotel, and are shaken hands with by Editor and myself. Official announcer does marvels in catching all their names and repeating them in superb shout. After every tenth name he diversifies things by adding, three semi-tones lower, *The Editor receiving*, which sounds like a Greek chorus, and is impressive.

Delightful interlude when I recognise dear Rose, with charming and beautifully dressed doctor friend from America, also Rose's niece--no reference made by either of us to Women's Institutes--the Principal from Mickleham Hall, of whom I hastily enquire as to Vicky's welfare and am told that she is quite well, and Very Good which is a relief,–and dear Angela, who is unfortunately just in time to catch this maternal reference, and looks superior. Regrettable, but undoubtedly human, aspiration crosses my mind that it would be agreeable to be seen by Lady B. in all this distinguished society, but she puts in no appearance, and have very little doubt that next time we meet I shall be riding a bicycle strung with parcels on way to the village, or at some similar disadvantage.

Soon after five o'clock I am told that We might go and have some tea now--which I do, and talk to many very agreeable strangers. Someone asks me Is Francis Iles here? and I have to reply that I do not know, and unknown woman suddenly joins in and assures me that Francis Iles is really Mr. Aldous Huxley, she happens to know. Am much impressed, and repeat this to several people, by way of showing that I possess inside information, but am disconcerted by unknown gentleman who tells me, in rather grave and censorious accents, that I am completely mistaken, as he happens to know that Francis Iles is in reality Miss Edith Sitwell. Give the whole thing up after this, and am presently told to take my seat on platform for Debate.

Quite abominable device has been instituted by which names of speakers are put into a hat, and drawn out haphazard, which means that none of us know when we are to speak except one gentleman who has--with admirable presence of mind--arranged to have a train to catch, so that he gets called upon at once.

Chairman does her duties admirably--justifies my insistence over and over again--speeches are excellent, and audience most appreciative.

Chairman--can she be doing it on purpose, from motives of revenge?–draws my name late in the day, and find myself obliged to follow after admirable and experienced speakers, who have already said everything that can possibly be said. Have serious thoughts of simulating a faint, but conscience intervenes, and I rise. Special Providence mercifully arranges that exactly as I do so I should meet the eye of American publisher, whom I know well and like. He looks encouraging--and I mysteriously find myself able to utter. Great relief when this is over.

Short speech from *Time and Tide*'s Editor brings down the house, and Debate is brought to a close by the Chairman.

Party definitely a success, and am impressed by high standard of charm, good looks, intelligence, and excellent manners of *Time and Tide* readers. Unknown and delightful lady approaches me, and says, without preliminary of any kind: How is Robert? which pleases me immensely, and propose to send him a post card about it to-night.

Am less delighted by another complete stranger, who eyes me rather coldly and observes that I am What She Calls Screamingly Funny. Cannot make up my mind if she is referring to my hat, my appearance generally, or my contributions to *Time and Tide*. Can only hope the latter.

Am offered a lift home in a taxi by extremely well-known novelist, which gratifies me, and hope secretly that as many people as possible see me go away with him, and know who he is--which they probably do--and who I am--which they probably don't.

Spend entire evening in ringing up everybody I can think of, to ask how they enjoyed the Party.

June 18th.–Heat-wave continues, and everyone says How lovely it must be in the country, but personally think it is lovely in London, and am more than content.

Write eloquent letter to Robert suggesting that he should come up too, and go with me to Robin's School Sports on June 25th and that we should take Vicky. Have hardly any hope that he will agree to any of this.

Rose's Viscountess--henceforth Anne to me--rings up, and says that she has delightful scheme by which Rose is to motor me on Sunday to place--indistinguishable on telephone--in Buckinghamshire, where delightful Hotel, with remarkably beautiful garden, exists, and where we are to meet Anne and collection of interesting literary friends for lunch. Adds flatteringly that it will be so delightful to meet me again--had meant to say this myself about her, but must now abandon it, being unable to think out paraphrase in time. Reply that I shall look forward to Sunday, and we ring off.

Debate question of clothes--wardrobe, as usual, is deficient--and finally decide on green coat and skirt if weather cool, and new flowered tussore if hot.

(Problem here concerned with head-gear, as hat suitable for flowered tussore too large and floppy for motoring, and all other smaller hats--amounting to two, and one cap--entirely wrong colour to go with tussore.)

Literary Agent takes me out to lunch--is very nice--suggests that a little work on my-part would be desirable. I agree and sit and write all the evening vigorously.

June 19th.–Really very singular day, not calculated to rank amongst more successful experiences of life. Am called for by dear Rose in car, and told to hold map open on my knee, which I do, but in spite of this we get lost several times and Rose shows tendency to drive round and round various villages called Chalfont. After saying repeatedly that I expect the others will be late too, and that Anyway we have time in hand, I judge it better to introduce variations to the effect that We can't be far off now, and What about asking? Rose reluctantly agrees, and we ask three people, two of whom are strangers in the district, and the third is sorry but could not say at all, it might be ahead of us, or on the other hand we might be coming away from it. At this Rose mutters expletives and I feel it best to be silent.

Presently three Boy Scouts are sighted, and Rose stops again and interrogates them. They prove very willing and produce a map, and giggle a good deal, and I decide that one of them is rather like Robin, and forget to listen to what they say. Rose, however, dashes on again, and I think with relief that we are now doing well, when violent exclamation breaks from her that We have passed that self-same church tower three times already. Am filled with horror--mostly at my own inferior powers of observation, as had no idea whatever that I had ever set eyes on church tower in my life before--and suggest madly that we ought to turn to the right, I think. Rose--she must indeed be desperate--follows this advice and in about three minutes we miraculously reach our destination, and find that it is two o'clock. Dining-room is discovered--entire party half-way through lunch, and obviously not in the least pleased to see us--which is perfectly natural, as eruptions of this kind destructive to continuity of conversation, always so difficult of achievement in any case. Everyone says we must be Starving, and egg-dish is recalled--eggs disagree with me and am obliged to say No and my neighbour enquires Oh, why? which is ridiculous, and great waste of time--and we speed through cold chicken and strawberries and then adjourn to garden, of which there are acres and acres, and everybody very enthusiastic except myself. Just as I select comfortable chair next to Anne--whom I have, after all, come to see--perfectly unknown couple surge up out of the blue, and are introduced as General and Mrs. St. Something--cannot catch what--and General immediately says Wouldn't I like to go round the garden? Have not strength of mind enough to reply baldly No I wouldn't, and he conducts me up and down steps and in and out of paths and at intervals we say Just look at those lupins! and That's a good splash of colour--but mostly he tells me about Lord Rothermere. Try not to betray that I have never yet been able to distinguish between Lord R. and Lord Beaverbrook. General St. ? evidently thinks ill of both, and I make assenting sounds and am inwardly perfectly certain that Anne's party is being amused at my progress. Can hear them in shrieks of laughter in different parts of garden, which I now perceive to be the size of Hampton Court, more or less.

Rose suddenly appears round a yew hedge, and I give her a look that I hope she appreciates, and we gradually work our way back via more lupins, to deck-chairs. Anne still sitting there, looking extraordinarily amused. General St. Something instantly says that his wife would so like to have a talk with me about books, she materialises at his elbow, and at once declares that she must show me the garden. I demur, on the ground of having seen it already, and she assures me breezily that it will well bear seeing twice, or even more often, and that she herself could never get tired of that Blaze of Colour.

We accordingly pursue blaze of colour, while Mrs. St. ? talks to me about poetry, which she likes and I don't, Siamese cats, that both of us like, and the lace-making industry.

Garden now definitely acquires dimensions of the Zoo at least, and I give up all hope of ever being allowed to sit down again. Can see Anne talking to Rose in the distance, and both appear to be convulsed with mirth.

Distant clock strikes four--should not have been surprised if it had been eight--and I break in on serious revelations about lack of rear-lights on bicycles in country districts, and say that I am perfectly certain I ought to be going. Civil regrets are exchanged--entirely hypocritical on my part, and probably on hers as well--and we walk about quarter of a mile and find Rose. Mrs. St. Something disappears (probably going round the garden again) and I am very angry indeed and say that I have never had such a day in all my life. Everybody else laughs heartily, and appears to feel that afternoon has been highly successful and Rose hysterically thanks Anne for inviting us. Make no pretence whatever of seconding this. Drive home is very much shorter than drive out, and I do not attempt to make myself either useful or agreeable in any way.

June 23rd.–Am pleased and astonished at being taken at my word by Robert, who appears at the flat, and undertakes to conduct me, and Vicky, to half-term Sports at Robin's school. In the meantime, he wants a hair-cut. I say that there is a place quite near Southampton Row, at which Robert looks appalled, and informs me that there is *No* place nearer than Bond Street. He accordingly departs to Bond Street, after telling me to meet him at twelve at his Club in St. James's. Am secretly much impressed by nonchalance with which Robert resumes these urban habits, although to my certain knowledge he has not been near Club in St. James's for years.

Reflection here on curious dissimilarity between the sexes as exemplified by self and Robert: in his place, should be definitely afraid of not being recognised by hall-porter of Club, and quite possibly challenged as to my right to be there at all. Robert, am perfectly well aware, will on the contrary ignore hall-porter from start to finish with probable result that h.-p. will crawl before him, metaphorically if not literally.

I CALL FOR ROBERT AT HIS CLUB

This rather interesting abstract speculation recurs to me with some violence when I actually do go to Club, and enter imposing-looking hall, presided over by still more imposing porter in uniform, to whom I am led up by compassionate-looking page, who evidently realises my state of inferiority. Am made no better by two elderly gentlemen talking together in a corner, both of whom look at me with deeply suspicious faces and evidently think I have designs on something or other--either the Club statuary, which is looming above me, or perhaps themselves? Page is despatched to look for Robert--feel as if my only friend had been taken from me--and I wait, in state of completely suspended animation, for what seems like a long week-end. This comes to an end at last, and am moved to greet Robert by extraordinary and totally unsuitable quotation: *Time and the hour runs through the roughest day*–which I hear myself delivering, in an inward voice, exactly as if I were talking in my sleep. Robert--on the whole wisely--takes not the faintest notice, beyond looking at me with rather an astonished expression, and receives his hat and coat, which page-boy presents as if they were Coronation robes and sceptre at the very least. We walk out of Club, and I resume customary control of my senses.

Day is one of blazing sunlight, streets thronged with people, and we walk along Piccadilly and Robert says Let's lunch at Simpson's in the Strand, to which I agree, and add Wouldn't it be heavenly if we were rich? Conversation then ensues on more or less accustomed lines, and we talk about school-bills, inelastic spirit shown by the Bank, probabilities that new house-parlourmaid will be giving notice within the next few weeks, and unlikelihood of our having any strawberries worth mentioning in the garden this year. Robert's contribution mostly consists of ejaculations about the traffic--he doesn't know what the streets are coming to, but it can't go on like this--and a curt assurance to the effect that we shall all be in the workhouse together before so very long. After this we reach Simpson's in the Strand, and Robert says that we may as well have a drink--which we do, and feel better.

Am impressed by Simpson's, where I have never been before, and lunch is agreeable. In the middle of it perceive Pamela Pringle, wearing little black-and-white hat exactly like old-fashioned pill-box, and not much larger, and extraordinarily effective black frock--also what looks like, and probably is, a collection of at least nine real-diamond bracelets. She is, needless to say, escorted by young gentleman, who looks totally unsuited to his present surroundings, as he has side-whiskers, a pale green face, and general aspect that reminds me immediately of recent popular song entitled: "My Canary has Circles under His Eyes".

Pamela deeply absorbed in conversation, but presently catches sight of me, and smiles--smile a very sad one, which is evidently tone of the interview--and then sees Robert, at which she looks more animated, and eventually gets up and comes towards us, leaving Canary with Circles under His Eyes throwing bits of bread about the table in highly morose and despairing fashion.

Robert is introduced; Pamela opens her eyes very widely and says she has heard so very much about him--(who from? Not me)–and they shake hands. Can see from Robert's expression exactly what he thinks of Pamela's finger-nails, which are vermilion. P. P. says that we must come and see her--can we dine together tonight, Waddell will be at home and one or two people are looking in afterwards?–No, we are very sorry, but this is impossible. Then Pamela will ring up this dear thing--evidently myself, but do not care about the description--and meanwhile she simply must go back. The boy she is lunching with is Hipps, the artist. Robert looks perfectly blank and I--not at all straightforwardly--assume an interested expression and say Oh really, as if I knew all about Hipps, and Pamela adds that the poor darling is all decadent and nervy, and she thought this place would do him good, but really he's in such a state that Paris is the only possible thing for him. She gives Robert her left hand, throws me a kiss with the other, and rejoins the Canary--whose face is now buried in his arms. Robert says Good God and asks why that woman doesn't wash that stuff off those nails. This question obviously rhetorical, and do not attempt any reply, but enquire if he thought Pamela pretty. Robert, rather strangely, makes sound which resembles Tchah! from which I deduce a negative, and am not as much distressed as I ought to be at this obvious injustice to P. P.'s face and figure. Robert follows this by further observation, this time concerning the Canary with Circles under His Eyes, which would undoubtedly lead to libel action, if not to charge of using obscene language in public, if overheard, and I say Hush, and make enquiries as to the well-being of Our Vicar and Our Vicar's Wife, in order to change the subject.

That reminds Robert: there is to be a concert in the Village next month for most deserving local object, and he has been asked to promise my services as performer, which he has done.

Definite conviction here that reference ought to be made to Married Women's Property Act or something like that, but exact phraseology eludes me, and Robert seems so confident that heart fails me, and I weakly agree to do what I can. (This, if taken literally, will amount to extraordinarily little, as have long ceased to play piano seriously, have never at any time been able to sing, and have completely forgotten few and amateurish recitations that have occasionally been forced upon me on local platforms.)

Plans for the afternoon discussed: Robert wishes to visit Royal Academy, and adds that he need not go and see his Aunt Mary as I went there the other day--which seems to me illogical, and altogether unjust--and that we will get stalls for to-night if I will say what play I want to see. After some thought, select *Musical Chairs*, mainly because James Agate has written well of it in the Press, and Robert says Good, he likes a musical show, and I have to explain that I don't think it is a musical show, at all, and we begin all over again, and finally select a revue. Debate question of Royal Academy, but have no inclination whatever to go there, and have just said so, as nicely as I can, when Pamela again appears beside us, puts her hand on Robert's shoulder--at which he looks startled and winces slightly--and announces that we *must* come to Hipps' picture-show this afternoon--it is in the Cygnet Galleries in Fitzroy Square, and if no one turns up it will break the poor pet's heart, and as far as she can see, no one but herself has ever heard of it, and we simply must go there, and help her out. She will meet us there at five.

Before we have recovered ourselves in any way, we are more or less committed to the Cygnet Galleries at five, Pamela has told us that she adores us both--but looks exclusively at Robert as she says it--and has left us again. Shortly afterwards, observe her paying bill for herself and the Canary, who is now drinking old brandy in reckless quantities.

Robert again makes use of expletives, and we leave Simpson's and go our several ways, but with tacit agreement to obey Pamela's behest. I fill in the interval with prosaic purchases of soap, which I see in mountainous heaps at much reduced prices, filling an entire shop-window, sweets to take down to Robin on Saturday, and quarter-pound of tea in order that Robert may have usual early-morning cup before coming out--unwillingly--to breakfast at Lyons'.

Am obliged to return to Doughty Street, and get small jug in which to collect milk from dairy in Gray's Inn Road, pack suitcase now in order to save time in the morning, and finally proceed to Fitzroy Square, where Cygnet Galleries are discovered, after some search, in small adjoining street which is not in Fitzroy Square at all.

Robert and the Canary are already together, in what I think really frightful juxtaposition, and very, very wild collection of pictures hangs against the walls. Robert and I walk round and round, resentfully watched by the Canary, who never stirs, and Pamela Pringle fails to materialise.

ROBERT IMBIBES CULTURE

Can think of nothing whatever to say, but mutter something about It's all being Very Interesting, from time to time, and at last come to a halt before altogether astonishing group that I think looks like a wedding--which is a clearer impression than I have managed to get of any of the other pictures. Am just wondering whether it is safe to take this for granted, when the Canary joins us, and am again stricken into silence. Robert, however, suddenly enquires If that is the League of Nations, to which the Canary, in a very hollow voice, says that he knows nothing whatever about the League of Nations, and I experience strong impulse to reply that we know nothing whatever about pictures, and that the sooner we part for ever, the better for us all.

This, however, is impossible, and feel bound to await Pamela, so go round the room all over again, as slowly as possible, only avoiding the wedding-group, to which no further reference is made by any of us. After some time of this, invisible telephone-bell rings, and the Canary--very curious writhing movement, as he walks--goes away to deal with it, and Robert says For God's sake let's get out of this. I ask Does he mean now this minute, and he replies Yes, before that morbid young owl comes back, and we snatch up our various possessions and rush out. The Canary, rather unfortunately, proves to be on the landing half-way downstairs, leaning against a wall and holding telephone receiver to his ear. He gives us a look of undying hatred as we go past, and the last we hear of him is his voice, repeating desperately down the telephone that Pamela *can't* do a thing like that, and fail him utterly--she absolutely can't. (Personally, am entirely convinced that she can, and no doubt will.)

Robert and I look at one another, and he says in a strange voice that he must have a drink, after that, and we accordingly go in search of it.

June 25th.–Vicky arrives by green bus from Mickleham, carrying circular hat-box of astonishing size and weight, with defective handle, so that every time I pick it up, it falls down again, which necessitates a taxi. She is in great excitement, and has to be calmed with milk and two buns before we proceed to station, meet Robert, and get into the train.

Arrival, lunch at Hotel, and walk up to School follow normal lines, and in due course Robin appears and is received by Vicky with terrific demonstrations of affection and enthusiasm, to which he responds handsomely. (Reflect, as often before, that Fashion in this respect has greatly altered. Brothers and sisters now almost universally deeply attached to one another, and quite prepared to admit it. *O temporal O mores!*) We are conducted to the playing-fields, where hurdles and other appliances of sports are ready, and where rows and rows of chairs await us.

Parents, most of whom I have seen before and have no particular wish ever to see again, are all over the place, and am once more struck by tendency displayed by all Englishwomen to cling to most unbecoming outfit of limp coat and skirt and felt hat even when blazing summer day demands cooler, and infinitely more becoming, *ensemble* of silk frock and shady hat.

Crowds of little boys all look angelic in running shorts and singlets, and am able to reflect that even if Robin's hair *is* perfectly straight, at least he doesn't wear spectacles.

Headmaster speaks a few words to me--mostly about the weather, and new wing that he proposes, as usual, to put up very shortly--I accost Robin's Form-master and demand to be told How the Boy is Getting On, and Form-master looks highly astonished at my audacity, and replies in a very off-hand way that Robin will never be a cricketer, but his football is coming on, and he has the makings of a swimmer. He then turns his back on me, but I persist, and go so far as to say that I should like to hear something about Robin's Work.

Form-master appears to be altogether overcome by this unreasonable requirement, and there is a perceptible silence, during which he evidently meditates flight. Do my best to hold him by the Power of the Human Eye, about which I have read much, not altogether believingly. However, on this occasion, it does its job, and Form-master grudgingly utters five words or so, to the effect that we needn't worry about Robin's Common-entrance exam. in two years' time. Having so far committed himself he pretends to see a small boy in imminent danger on a hurdle and dashes across the grass at uttermost speed to save him, and for the remainder of the day, whenever he finds himself within yards of me, moves rapidly in opposite direction.

Sports take place, and are a great success. Robin murmurs to me that he thinks, he isn't at all sure, but he *thinks*, he may have a chance in the High Jump. I reply, with complete untruth, that I shan't mind a bit if he doesn't win and he mustn't be disappointed--and then suffer agonies when event actually takes place and he and another boy out-jump everybody else and are at last declared to have tied. (Vicky has to be rebuked by Robert for saying that this is Unjust and Robin jumped by far the best--which is not only an unsporting attitude, but entirely unsupported by fact.) Later in the afternoon Robin comes in a good second in Hurdling, and Vicky is invited to take part in a three-legged race, which she does with boundless enthusiasm and no skill at all.

Tea and ices follow--boys disappear, and are said to be changing--and I exchange remarks with various parents, mostly about the weather being glorious, the sports well organised, and the boys a healthy-looking lot.

Trophies are distributed--inclination to tears, of which I am violently ashamed, assails me when Robin goes up to receive two little silver cups--various people cheer various other people, and we depart for the Hotel, with Robin. Evening entirely satisfactory, and comes to an end at nine o'clock, with bed for Vicky and Robin's return to school.

June 27th.–Return to London, departure of Vicky by green bus and under care of the conductor, and of Robert from Paddington. I have assured him that I shall be home in a very few days now, and he has again reminded me about the concert, and we part. Am rung up by Pamela in the afternoon, to ask if I can bring Robert to tea, and have great satisfaction in informing her that he has returned to Devonshire. Pamela then completely takes the wind out of my sails by saying that she will be motoring through Devonshire quite soon, and would simply love to look us up. A really very interesting man who Rows will be with her, and she thinks that we should like to know him. Social exigencies compel me to reply that of course we should, and I hope she will bring her rowing friend to lunch or tea whenever she is in the neighbourhood.

After this, permit myself to enquire why P. P. never turned up at Cygnet Galleries on recent painful occasion; to which she answers, in voice of extreme distress, that I simply can't imagine how complicated life is, and men give one no peace at all, and it's so difficult when one friend hates another friend and threatens to shoot him if Pamela goes out with him again.

Am obliged to admit that attitude of this kind does probably lead to very involved situations, and Pamela says that I am so sweet and understanding, always, and I must give that angel Robert her love--and rings off.

June 29th.–Am filled with frantic desire to make the most of few remaining days in London, and recklessly buy two pairs of silk stockings, for no other reason than that they catch my eye when on my way to purchase sponge-bag and tooth-paste for Vicky.

(*Query:* Does sponge-bag exist anywhere in civilised world which is positively water-proof and will not sooner or later exude large, damp patches from sponge that apparently went into it perfectly dry? Secondary, but still important, *Query:* Is it possible to reconcile hostile attitude invariably exhibited by all children towards process of teeth-cleaning with phenomenal rapidity with which they demolish tube after tube of tooth-paste?)

Proceed later to small and newly established Registry Office, which has been recommended to me by Felicity, and am interviewed by lady in white satin blouse, who tells me that maids for the country are almost impossible to find--which I know very well already--but that she will do what she can for me, and I mustn't mind if it's only an inexperienced girl. I agree not to mind, provided the inexperienced girl is willing to learn, and not expensive, and white-satin blouse says Oh dear yes, to the first part, and Oh dear no, to the second, and then turns out to have twenty-five shillings a week in mind, at which I protest, and we are obliged to begin all over again, on totally different basis. She finally dismisses me, with pessimistic hopes that I may hear from her in the next few days, and demand for a booking-fee, which I pay.

Return to Doughty Street, where I am rung up by quite important daily paper and asked If I would care to write an Article about Modern Freedom in Marriage. First impulse is to reply that they must have made a mistake, and think me more celebrated than I am--but curb this, and ask how long article would have to be--really meaning what is the shortest they will take--and how much they are prepared to pay? They--represented by brisk and rather unpleasant voice--suggest fifteen hundred words, and a surprisingly handsome fee. Very well then, I will do it--how soon do they want it? Voice replies that early next week will be quite all right, and we exchange good-byes. Am highly exhilarated, decide to give a dinner-party, pay several bills, get presents for the children, take them abroad in the summer holidays, send Robert a cheque towards pacifying the Bank, and buy myself a hat. Realise, however, that article is not yet written, far less paid for, and that the sooner I collect my ideas about Modern Freedom in Marriage, the better.

Just as I have got ready to do so, interruption comes in the person of Housekeeper from upstairs, who Thinks that I would like to see the laundry-book. I do see it, realise with slight shock that it has been going on briskly for some weeks unperceived by myself, and produce the necessary sum. Almost immediately afterwards a Man comes to the door, and tells me that I have no doubt often been distressed by the dirty and unhygienic condition of my telephone. Do not like to say that I have never thought about it, so permit him to come in, shake his head at the telephone, and say Look at that, now, and embark on long and alarming monologue about Germs. By the time he has finished, realise that I am lucky to be alive at all in midst of numerous and insidious perils, and agree to telephone's being officially disinfected at stated intervals. Form, as usual, has to be filled up, Man then delivers parting speech to the effect that he is very glad I've decided to do this--there's so many ladies don't realise, and if they knew what they was exposing themselves to, they'd be the first to shudder at it--which sounds like White Slave Traffic, but is, I think, still Germs. I say Well, Good-morning, and he replies rebukefully--and correctly--Good afternoon, which I feel bound to accept by repeating it after him, and he goes downstairs.

I return to Modern Freedom in Marriage and get ready to deal with it by sharpening a pencil and breaking the lead three times. Extremely violent knock at flat door causes me to drop it altogether--(fourth and absolutely final break)–and admit very powerful-looking window-cleaner with pair of steps, mop, bucket and other appliances, all of which he hurls into the room with great *abandon.* I say Will he begin with the bedroom, and he replies that it's all one to him, and is temporarily lost to sight in next room, but can be heard singing: *I Don't Know Why I Love You Like I Do.* (Remaining lines of this idyll evidently unknown to him as he repeats this one over and over again, but must in justice add that he sings rather well.)

Settle down in earnest to Modern Freedom in Marriage. Draw a windmill on blotting-paper. Tell myself that a really striking opening sentence is important. Nothing else matters. Really striking sentence is certainly hovering somewhere about, although at the moment elusive. (*Query:* Something about double standard of morality? Or is this unoriginal? Thread temporarily lost, owing to absorption in shading really admirable little sketch of Cottage Loaf drawn from Memory...)

Frightful crash from bedroom, and abrupt cessation of not Knowing Why He Loves Me Like He Does, recalls window-cleaner with great suddenness to my mind, and I open door that separates us and perceive that he has put very stalwart arm clean through windowpane and is bleeding vigorously, although, with great good feeling, entirely avoiding carpet or furniture.

Look at him in some dismay, and enquire--not intelligently--if he is hurt, and he answers No, the cords were wore clean through, it happens sometimes with them old-fashioned sashes. Rather singular duet follows, in which I urge him to come and wash his arm in the kitchen, and he completely ignores the suggestion and continues to repeat that the cords were wore clean through. After a good deal of this, I yield temporarily, look at the cords and agree that they do seem to be wore clean through, and finally hypnotise window-cleaner--still talking about the cords--into following me to the sink, where he holds his arm under cold water and informs me that the liability of his company is strictly limited, so far as the householder is concerned, and in my case the trouble was due to them cords being practically wore right through.

I enquire if his arm hurts him--at which he looks blankly astonished--inspect the cut, produce iodine and apply it, and finally return to Modern Freedom in Marriage, distinctly shattered, whilst window-cleaner resumes work, but this time without song.

Literary inspiration more and more evasive every moment, and can think of nothing whatever about Modern Freedom except that it doesn't exist in the provinces. Ideas as to Marriage not lacking, but these would certainly not be printed by any newspaper on earth, and should myself be deeply averse from recording them in any way.

Telephone rings and I instantly decide that: (a) Robert has died suddenly. (b) Literary Agent has effected a sale of my film-rights, recent publication, for sum running into five figures, pounds not dollars. (c) Robin has met with serious accident at school. (d) Pamela Pringle wishes me once more to cover her tracks whilst engaged in pursuing illicit amour of one kind or another.

(*Note:* Swiftness of human (female) imagination surpasses that of comet's trail across the heavens quite easily. Could not this idea be embodied in short poem? Am convinced, at the moment, that some such form of expression would prove infinitely easier than projected article about Modern Freedom, etc.)

I say Yes? into the telephone--entire flight of fancy has taken place between two rings--and unknown contralto voice says that I shan't remember her--which is true--but that she is Helen de Liman de la Pelouse and we met at Pamela Pringle's at lunch one day last October. To this I naturally have to reply Oh yes, yes--indeed we did--as if it all came back to me--which it does, in a way, only cannot possibly remember anything except collection of women all very much better dressed and more socially competent than myself, and am perfectly certain that H. de L. de la P. was never introduced by name at all. (Would probably have taken too long, in crowded rush of modern life.)

Will I forgive last-minute invitation and come and dine to-night and meet one or two people, all interested in Books, and H. de la P.'s cousin, noted literary critic whom I may like to know? Disturbing implication here that literary critics allow their judgment to be influenced by considerations other than aesthetic and academic ones--but cannot unravel at the moment, and merely accept with pleasure and say What time and Where? Address in large and expensive Square is offered me, time quarter to nine if that isn't too late? (*Query:* What would happen, if I said Yes, it is too late? Would entire scheme be reorganised?)

Am recalled from this rather idle speculation by window-cleaner--whose very existence I have completely forgotten--taking his departure noisily, but with quite unresentful salutation, and warning--evidently kindly intended--that them cords are wore through and need seeing to. I make a note on the blotting-paper to this effect, and am again confronted with perfectly blank sheet of paper waiting to receive masterpiece of prose concerning Modern Freedom in Marriage. Decide that this is definitely not the moment to deal with it, and concentrate instead on urgent and personal questions concerned with to-night's festivity. Have practically no alternative as to frock--recently acquired silver brocade--and hair has fortunately been shampoo'd and set within the last three days so still looks its best--evening cloak looks well when on, and as it will remain either in hall or hostess's bedroom, condition of the lining need concern no one but myself and servant in attendance--who will be obliged to keep any views on the subject concealed. Shoes will have to be reclaimed immediately from the cleaners, but this easily done. More serious consideration is that of taxi-fare, absolutely necessitated by situation of large and expensive Square, widely removed from bus or tube routes. Am averse from cashing cheque, for very sound reason that balance is at lowest possible ebb and recent passages between Bank and myself give me no reason to suppose that they will view even minor overdraft with indulgence--and am only too well aware that shopping expedition and laundry-book between them have left me with exactly fivepence in hand.

Have recourse, not for the first time, to perhaps rather infantile, but by no means unsuccessful, stratagem of unearthing small hoards of coins distributed by myself, in more affluent moments, amongst all the hand-bags I possess in the world.

Two sixpences, some halfpence, one florin and a half-crown are thus brought to light, and will see me handsomely through the evening, and breakfast at Lyons' next morning into the bargain.

Am unreasonably elated by this and go so far as to tell myself that very likely I shall collect some ideas for Modern Freedom article in general conversation to-night and needn't bother about it just now.

Rose comes in unexpectedly, and is immediately followed by Felicity Fairmead, but they do not like one another and atmosphere lacks *entrain* altogether. Make rather spasmodic conversation about the children, *The Miracle*–which we all three of us remember perfectly well in the old days at Olympia, but all declare severally that we were more or less children at the time and too young to appreciate it--and State of Affairs in America, which we agree is far worse than it is here. This is openly regretted by Rose (because she knows New York well and enjoyed being there) and by me (because I have recently met distinguished American publisher and liked him very much) and rejoiced in by Felicity (because she thinks Prohibition is absurd). Feminine mentality rather curiously and perhaps not altogether creditably illustrated here. Have often wondered on exactly what grounds I am a Feminist, and am sorry to say that no adequate reply whatever presents itself. Make note to think entire question out dispassionately when time permits--if it ever does.

Rose and Felicity both refuse my offer of tea and mixed biscuits--just as well, as am nearly sure there is no milk--and show strong inclination to look at one another expectantly in hopes of an immediate departure. Rose gives in first, and goes, and directly she has left Felicity asks me what on earth I see in her, but does not press for an answer. We talk about clothes, mutual friends, and utter impossibility of keeping out of debt. Felicity--who is, and always has been, completely unworldly, generous and utterly childlike--looks at me with enormous brown eyes, and says solemnly that nothing in this world--NOTHING--matters except Money, and on this she takes her departure. I empty cigarette ash out of all the ash-trays--Felicity doesn't smoke at all and Rose and I only had one cigarette each, but results out of all proportion--and go through customary far-sighted procedure of turning down bed, drawing curtains and filling kettle for hot-water bottle, before grappling with geyser, of which I am still mortally terrified, and getting ready for party. During these operations I several times encounter sheet of paper destined to record my views about Modern Freedom in Marriage, but do nothing whatever about it, except decide again how I shall spend the money.

Am firmly resolved against arriving too early, and do not telephone for taxi until half-past eight, then find number engaged, and operator--in case of difficulty dial 0--entirely deaf to any appeal. Accordingly rush out into the street--arrangement of hair suffers rather severely--find that I have forgotten keys and have to go back again--make a second attack on telephone, this time with success, rearrange coiffure and observe with horror that three short minutes in the open air are enough to remove every trace of powder from me, repair this, and depart at last.

After all this, am, as usual, first person to arrive. Highly finished product of modern civilisation, in white satin with no back and very little front, greets me, and I perceive her to be extremely beautiful, and possessed of superb diamonds and pearls. Evidently Helen de Liman de la Pelouse. This conjecture confirmed when she tells me, in really very effective drawl, that we sat opposite to one another at Pamela Pringle's luncheon party, and may she introduce her husband? Husband is apparently Jewish--why de Liman de la Pelouse?–and looks at me in a rather lifeless and exhausted way and then gives me a glass of sherry, evidently in the hope of keeping me quiet. H. de L. de la P. talks about the weather--May very wet, June very hot, English climate very uncertain--and husband presently joins in and says all the same things in slightly different words. We then all three look at one another in despair, until I am suddenly inspired to remark that I have just paid a most interesting visit to the studio of a rather interesting young man whose work I find interesting, called Hipps. (Should be hard put to it to say whether construction of this sentence, or implication that it conveys, is the more entirely alien to my better principles.) Experiment proves immediately successful, host and hostess become animated, and H. de L. de la P. says that Hipps is quite the most mordant of the younger set of young present-day satirists, don't I think, and that last thing of his definitely had *patine*. I recklessly agree, but am saved from further perjury by arrival of more guests. All are unknown to me, and fill me with terror, but pretty and harmless creature in black comes and stands next me, and we talk about *1066 and All That* and I say that if I'd known in time that the authors were schoolmasters I should have sent my son to them at all costs, and she says Oh, have I children?–but does not, as I faintly hope, express any surprise at their being old enough to go to school at all--and I say Yes, two, and then change the subject rather curtly for fear of becoming involved in purely domestic conversation.

Find myself at dinner between elderly man with quantities of hair, and much younger man who looks nice and smiles at me. Make frantic endeavours, without success, to read names on little cards in front of them, and wish violently that I ever had sufficient presence of mind to listen to people's names when introduced--which I never do.

Try the elderly man with Hipps. He does not respond. Switch over to thinking he knows a friend of mine, Mrs. Pringle? No, he doesn't think so. Silence follows, and I feel it is his turn to say something, but as he doesn't, and as my other neighbour is talking hard to pretty woman in black, I launch into Trade Depression and Slump in America, and make a good deal of use of all the more intelligent things said by Rose and Felicity this afternoon. Elderly neighbour still remains torpid except for rather caustic observation concerning Mr. Hoover. Do not feel competent to defend Mr. Hoover, otherwise should certainly do so, as by this time am filled with desire to contradict everything elderly neighbour may ever say. He gives me, however, very little opportunity for doing so, as he utters hardly at all and absorbs himself in perfectly admirable lobster *Thermidor*. Final effort on my part is to tell him the incident of the window-cleaner, which I embroider very considerably in rather unsuccessful endeavour to make it amusing, and this at last unseals his lips and he talks quite long and eloquently about Employers' Liability, which he views as an outrage. Consume lobster silently, in my turn, and disagree with him root and branch, but feel that it would be waste of time to say so and accordingly confine myself to invaluable phrase: I See What He Means.

We abandon mutual entertainment with great relief shortly afterwards, and my other neighbour talks to me about books, says that he has read mine and proves it by a quotation, and I decide that he must be distinguished critic spoken of by H. de L. de la P. Tell him the story of window-cleaner, introducing several quite new variations, and he is most encouraging, laughs heartily, and makes me feel that I am a witty and successful *raconteuse*–which in saner moments I know very well that I am not.

(*Query:* Has this anything to do with the champagne? *Answer*, almost certainly, Yes, everything.)

Amusing neighbour and myself continue to address one another exclusively--fleeting wonder as to what young creature in black feels about me--and am sorry when obliged to ascend to drawing-room for customary withdrawal. Have a feeling that H. de L. de la P.–who eyes me anxiously--is thinking that I am Rather A Mistake amongst people who all know one another very well indeed. Try to tell myself that this is imagination, and all will be easier when drinking coffee, which will not only give me occupation--always a help--but clear my head, which seems to be buzzing slightly.

H. de L. de la P. refers to Pamela--everybody in the room evidently an intimate friend of Pamela's, and general galvanisation ensues. *Isn't* she adorable? says very smart black-and-white woman, and Doesn't that new platinum hair suit her too divinely? asks somebody else, and we all cry Yes, quite hysterically, to both. H. de L. de la P. then points me out and proclaims--having evidently found a *raison d' etre* for me at last--that I have known Pamela for years and years--longer than any of them. I instantly become focus of attention, and everyone questions me excitedly.

Do I know what became of the *second* husband?–Templer-Something was his name. No explanation ever forthcoming of his disappearance, and immediate replacement by somebody else. Have I any idea of Pamela's real age? Of course she looks too, too marvellous, but it is an absolute fact that her eldest child can't possibly be less than fifteen, and it was the child of the second marriage, *not* the first.

Do I know anything about that Pole who used to follow her about everywhere, and was supposed to have been shot by his wife in Paris on account of P. P.?

Is it true that Pringle--unfortunate man--isn't going to stand it any longer and has threatened to take Pamela out to Alaska to live?

And is she--poor darling--still going about with the second husband of that woman she's such friends with?

Supply as many answers as I can think of to all this, and am not perturbed as to their effect, feeling perfectly certain that whatever I say Pamela's dear friends have every intention of believing, and repeating, whatever they think most sensational and nothing else.

This conviction intensified when they, in their turn, overwhelm me with information.

Do I realise, says phenomenally slim creature with shaven eyebrows, that Pamela will really get herself into difficulties one of these days, if she isn't more careful? That, says the eyebrows--impressively, but surely inaccurately--is Pamela's trouble. She isn't *careful*. Look at the way she behaved with that South American millionaire at Le Touquet!

Look, says somebody else, at her affair with the Prince. Reckless--no other word for it.

Finally H. de L. de la P.–who has been quietly applying lip-stick throughout the conversation--begs us all to Look at the *type* of man that falls for Pamela. She knows that Pamela is attractive, of course--sex-appeal, and all that--but after all, that can't go on for ever, and then what will be left? Nothing whatever. Pamela's men aren't the kind to go on being devoted. They simply have this brief flare-up, and then drift off to something younger and newer. Every time. Always.

Everybody except myself agrees, and several people look rather relieved about it. Conversation closes, as men are heard upon the stairs, with H. de L. de la P. assuring us all that Pamela is one of her very dearest friends, and she simply adores her--which is supported by assurances of similar devotion from everyone else. Remain for some time afterwards in rather stunned condition, thinking about Friendship, and replying quite mechanically, and no doubt unintelligently, to thin man who stands near me--(wish he would sit, am getting crick in my neck)–and talks about a drawing in *Punch* of which he thought very highly, but cannot remember if it was Raven Hill or Bernard Partridge, nor what it was about, except that it had something to do with Geneva.

Evening provides no further sensation, and am exceedingly sleepy long before somebody in emeralds and platinum makes a move. Pleasant man who sat next me at dinner has hoped, in agreeable accents, that we shall meet again--I have echoed the hope, but am aware that it has no foundation in probability--and H. de L. de la P. has said, at parting, that she is so glad I have had an opportunity of meeting her cousin, very well known critic. Do not like to tell her that I have never identified this distinguished *littérateur* at all, and leave the house still uninformed as to whether he was, or was not, either of my neighbours at dinner. Shall probably now never know.

July 1st.–Once more prepare to leave London, and am haunted by words of out-of-date song once popular: *How're you Going to Keep' em Down on the Farm, Now that they've seen Paree?* Answer comes there none.

Day filled with various activities, including packing, which I dislike beyond anything on earth and do very badly--write civil letter to H. de L. de la P. to say that I enjoyed her dinner-party, and ring up Rose in order to exchange good-byes. Rose, as usual, is out--extraordinary gadabout dear Rose is--and I leave rather resentful message with housekeeper, and return to uncongenial task of folding garments in sheets of tissue paper that are always either much too large or a great deal too small.

Suitcase is reluctant to close, I struggle for some time and get very hot, success at last, and am then confronted by neatly folded dressing-gown which I have omitted to put in.

Telephone rings and turns out to be Emma Hay, who is very very excited about satire which she says she has just written and which will set the whole of London talking. If I care to come round at once, says Emma, she is reading it aloud to a few Really Important People, and inviting free discussion and criticism afterwards.

I express necessary regrets, and explain that I am returning to the country in a few hours' time.

What, shrieks Emma, *leaving London?* Am I mad? Do I intend to spend the whole of the rest of my life pottering about the kitchen, and seeing that Robert gets his meals punctually, and that the children don't bring muddy boots into the house? Reply quite curtly and sharply: Yes, I Do, and ring off--which seems to me, on the whole, the quickest and most rational method of dealing with Emma.

July 4th.–Return home has much to recommend it, country looks lovely, everything more or less in bloom, except strawberries, which have unaccountably failed, Robert gives me interesting information regarding recent sale of heifer, and suspected case of sclerosis of the liver amongst neighbouring poultry, and Helen Wills claws at me demonstratively under the table as I sit down to dinner. Even slight *faux pas* on my own part, when I exclaim joyfully that the children will be home in a very short time now, fails to create really serious disturbance of harmonious domestic atmosphere.

Shall certainly not, in view of all this, permit spirits to be daunted by rather large pile of letters almost all concerned with Accounts Rendered, that I find on my writing-table. Could have dispensed, however, with the Milk-book, the Baker's Bill, and the Grocer's Total for the Month, all of them handed to me by Cook with rider to the effect that There was twelve-and-sixpence had to be given to the sweep, and twopence to pay on a letter last Monday week, and she hopes she did right in taking it in.

Robert enquires very amiably what I have been writing lately, and I say lightly, Oh, an article on Modern Freedom in Marriage, and then remember that I haven't done a word of it, and ask Robert to give me some ideas. He does so, and they are mostly to the effect that People talk a great deal of Rubbish nowadays, and that Divorce may be All Very Well in America, and the Trouble with most women is that they haven't got nearly Enough to Do. At this I thank Robert very much and say that will do splendidly--which is true in the spirit, though not the letter--but he appears to be completely wound up and unable to stop, and goes on for quite a long time, telling me to Look at Russia, and wishing to know How I should like to see the children whisked off to Siberia--which I think forceful but irrelevant.

Become surprisingly sleepy at ten o'clock--although this never happened to me in London--and go up to bed.

Extraordinary and wholly undesirable tendency displays itself to sit upon window-seat and think about Myself--but am well aware that this kind of thing never a real success, and that it will be the part of wisdom to get up briskly instead and look for shoe-trees to insert in evening-shoes--which I accordingly do; and shortly afterwards find myself in bed and ready to go to sleep.

July 8th.–Short, but rather poignant article on Day-Dreaming which appears in to-day's *Time and Tide* over signature of L. A. G. Strong, strangely bears out entry in my diary previous to this one. Am particularly struck--not altogether agreeably, either--by Mr. Strong's assertion that: "Day-dreaming is only harmful when it constitutes a mental rebellion against the circumstances of our life, which does not tend to any effort to improve them".

This phrase, quite definitely, exactly epitomises mental exercise in which a large proportion of my life is passed. Have serious thoughts of writing to Mr. Strong, and asking him what, if anything, can be done about it--but morning passes in telephone conversation with the Fish-middle-cut too expensive, what about a nice sole?–post card to Cissie Crabbe, in return for view of Scarborough with detached enquiry on the back as to How I am and How the children are--other post cards to tradespeople, cheque to the laundry, cheque to Registry Office, and cheque to local newsagent--and Mr. Strong is superseded. Nevertheless am haunted for remainder of the day by recollection surging up at unexpected moments, of the harmfulness of daydreams. Foresee plainly that this will continue to happen to me at intervals throughout the rest of life.

Just before lunch Our Vicar's Wife calls, and says that It's too bad to disturb me, and she has only just popped in for one moment and has to nip off to the school at once, but she did so want to talk to me about the concert, and hear all about London. Rather tedious and unnecessary argument follows as to whether she will or will not stay to lunch, and ends--as I always knew it would--in my ringing bell and saying Please lay an extra place for lunch, at the same time trying to send silent telepathic message to Cook that meat-pie alone will now not be enough, and she must do something with eggs or cheese as first course.

(Cook's interpretation of this subsequently turns out to be sardines, faintly grilled, lying on toast, which I think a mistake, but shall probably not say so, as intentions good.)

Our Vicar's Wife and I then plunge into the concert, now only separated from us by twenty-four hours. What, says Our Vicar's Wife hopefully, am I giving them? Well--how would it be if I gave them "John Gilpin"? (Know it already and shall not have to learn anything new.) Splendid, perfectly splendid, Our Vicar's Wife asserts in rather unconvinced accents. The only thing is, Didn't I give it to them at Christmas, and two years ago at the Church Organ Fête, and, unless she is mistaken, the winter before that again when we got up that entertainment for St. Dunstan's?

If this is indeed fact, obviously scheme requires revision. What about "An Austrian Army"? "An Austrian Army?" says Our Vicar's Wife. Is that the League of Nations?

(Extraordinary frequency with which the unfamiliar is always labelled the League of Nations appalls me.)

I explain that it is very, very interesting example of Alliterative Poetry, and add thoughtfully: "Apt Alliteration's Artful Aid", at which Our Vicar's Wife looks astounded, and mutters something to the effect that I mustn't be too clever for the rest of the world.

Conversation temporarily checked, and I feel discouraged, and am relieved when gong rings. This, however, produces sudden spate of protests from Our Vicar's Wife, who says she really must be off, she couldn't dream of staying to lunch, and what can she have been thinking of all this time?

Entrance of Robert--whose impassive expression on being unexpectedly confronted with a guest I admire--gives fresh turn to entire situation, and we all find ourselves in dining-room quite automatically.

Conversation circles round the concert, recent arrivals at neighbouring bungalow, on whom we all say that we must call, and distressing affair in the village which has unhappily ended by Mrs. A. of Jubilee Cottages being summonsed for assault by her neighbour Mrs. H. Am wholeheartedly thrilled by this, and pump Our Vicar's Wife for details, which she gives spasmodically, but has to switch off into French, or remarks about the weather, whenever parlour-maid is in the room.

Cook omits to provide coffee--in spite of definite instructions always to do so when we have a guest--and have to do the best I can with cigarettes, although perfectly well aware that Our Vicar's Wife does not smoke, and never has smoked.

Concert appears on the *tapis* once more, and Robert is induced to promise that he will announce the items. Our Vicar's Wife, rather nicely, says that everyone would love it if dear little Vicky could dance for us, and I reply that she will still be away at school, and Our Vicar's Wife replies that she knows *that*, she only meant how nice it would be if she *hadn't* been away at school, and could have danced for us. Am ungrateful enough to reflect that this is as singularly pointless an observation as ever I heard.

What, asks Our Vicar's Wife, am I doing this afternoon? Why not come with her and call on the new people at the bungalow and get it over? In this cordial frame of mind we accordingly set out, and I drive Standard car, Our Vicar's Wife observing--rather unnecessarily--that it really is *wonderful* how that car goes on and on and on.

THE GARDENING FAMILY

Conversation continues, covering much ground that has been traversed before, and only diversified by hopes from me that the bungalow inhabitants may all be out, and modification from Our Vicar's Wife to the effect that she is hoping to get them to take tickets for the concert.

Aspirations as to absence of new arrivals dashed on the instant of drawing up at their gate, as girl in cretonne overall, older woman--probably mother--with spectacles, and man in tweeds, are all gardening like mad at the top of the steps. They all raise themselves from stooping postures, and all wipe their hands on their clothes--freakish resemblance here to not very well co-ordinated revue chorus--and make polite pretence of being delighted to see us. Talk passionately about rock-gardens for some time, then are invited to come indoors, which we do, but cretonne overall and man in tweeds--turns out to be visiting uncle--sensibly remain behind and pursue their gardening activities.

We talk about the concert--two one-and-sixpenny tickets disposed of successfully--hostess reveals that she thinks sparrows have been building in one of the water-pipes, and I say Yes, they do do that, and Our Vicar's Wife backs me up, and shortly afterwards we take our leave.

On passing through village, Our Vicar's Wife says that we may just as well look in on Miss Pankerton, as she wants to speak to her about the concert. I protest, but to no avail, and we walk up Miss P.'s garden-path and hear her practising the violin indoors, and presently she puts her head out of ground-floor window and shrieks--still practising--that we are to walk straight in, which we do, upon which she throws violin rather recklessly on to the sofa--which is already piled with books, music, newspapers, appliances for raffia-work, garden-hat, hammer, chisel, sample tin of biscuits, and several baskets--and shakes us by both hands. She also tells me that she sees I have taken her advice, and released a good many of my inhibitions in that book of mine. Should like to deny violently having ever taken any advice of Miss P.'s at all, or even noticed that she'd given it, but she goes on to say that I ought to pay more attention to Style--and I diverge into wondering inwardly whether she means prose, or clothes.

(If the latter, this is incredible audacity, as Miss P.'s own costume--on broiling summer's day--consists of brick-red cloth dress, peppered with glass knobs, and surmounted by abominable little brick-red three-tiered cape, closely fastened under her chin.)

Our Vicar's Wife again launches out into the concert--has Miss P. an *encore* ready? Yes, she has. Two, if necessary. She supposes genially that I am giving a reading of some little thing of my own--I reply curtly that I am not, and shouldn't dream of such a thing--and Our Vicar's Wife, definitely tactful, interrupts by saying that She Hears Miss P. is off to London directly the concert is over. If this is really so, and it isn't giving her any trouble, could she and would she just look in at Harrods', where they are having a sale, and find out what about tinned apricots? Any reduction on a quantity, and how about carriage? And while she's in that neighbourhood--but not if it puts her out in any way--could she just look in at that little shop in the Fulham Road--the name has escaped Our Vicar's 'Wife for the moment--but it's really quite unmistakable--where they sell bicycle-parts? Our Vicar has lost a nut, quite a small nut, but rather vital, and it simply can't be replaced. Fulham Road the last hope.

Miss P.–I think courageously--undertakes it all, and writes down her London address, and Our Vicar's Wife writes down everything she can remember about Our Vicar's quite small nut, and adds on the same piece of paper the word "haddock".

But this, she adds, is only if Miss P. really *has* got time, and doesn't mind bringing it down with her, as otherwise it won't be fresh, only it does make a change and is so very difficult to get down here unless one is a regular customer.

At this point I intervene, and firmly suggest driving Our Vicar's Wife home, as feel certain that, if I don't, she will ask Miss P. to bring her a live crocodile from the Zoo, or something equally difficult of achievement.

We separate, with light-hearted anticipations of meeting again at the concert.

July 10th.–Concert permeates the entire day, and I spend at least an hour looking through *A Thousand and One Gems* and *The Drawing-room Reciter* in order to discover something that I once knew and can recapture without too much difficulty. Finally decide on narrative poem about Dick Turpin, unearthed in *Drawing-room Reciter*, and popular in far-away schooldays. Walk about the house with book in my hand most of the morning, and ask Robert to Hear Me after lunch, which he does, and only has to prompt three times. He handsomely offers to Hear Me again after tea, and to prompt if necessary during performance, and I feel that difficulty has been overcome.

Everything subject to interruption: small children arrive to ask if I can possibly lend them Anything Chinese, and am able to produce two paper fans--obviously made in Birmingham--one cotton kimono--eight-and-eleven at Messrs. Frippy and Coleman's--and large nautilus shell, always said to have been picked up by remote naval ancestor on the shore at Hawaii.

They express themselves perfectly satisfied, I offer them toffee, which they accept, and they depart with newspaper parcel. Later on message comes from the Rectory, to say that my contribution to Refreshments has not arrived, am covered with shame, and sacrifice new ginger-cake just made for to-day's tea.

Concert, in common with every other social activity in the village, starts at 7.30, and as Robert has promised to Take the Door and I am required to help with arranging the platform, we forgo dinner altogether, and eat fried fish at tea, and Robert drinks a whisky-and-soda.

Rumour has spread that Our Member and his wife are to appear at concert, but on my hoping this is true, since both are agreeable people, Robert shakes his head and says there's nothing in it. Everyone else, he admits, will be there, but *not* Our Member and his wife. I resign myself, and we both join in hoping that we shan't have to sit next Miss Pankerton. This hope realised, as Robert is put at the very end of front row of chairs, in order that he may get off and on platform frequently, and I am next him and have Our Vicar's Wife on my other side.

I ask for Our Vicar, and am told that his hay-fever has come on worse than ever, and he has been persuaded to stay at home. Regretful reference is made to this by Robert from the platform, and concert begins, as customary, with piano duet between Miss F. from the shop, and Miss W. of the smithy.

Have stipulated that Dick Turpin is to come on very early, so as to get it over, and am asked by Our Vicar's Wife if I am nervous. I say Yes, I am, and she is sympathetic, and tells me that the audience will be indulgent. They are, and Dick Turpin is safely accomplished with only one prompt from Robert--unfortunately delivered rather loudly just as I am purposely making what I hope is pregnant and dramatic pause--and I sit down again and prepare to enjoy myself.

Miss Pankerton follows me, is accompanied by pale young man who loses his place twice, and finally drops his music on the ground, picks it up again and readjusts it, while Miss P. glares at him and goes on vigorously with *Une Fête à Trianon* and leaves him to find his own way home as best he can. This he never quite succeeds in doing until final chord is reached, when he joins in again with an air of great triumph, and we all applaud heartily.

Miss P. bows, and at once launches into *encore*–which means that everybody else will have to be asked for an *encore* too, otherwise there will be feelings--and eventually sits down again and we go on to Sketch by the school-children, in which paper fans and cotton kimonos are in evidence.

The children look nice, and are delighted with themselves, and everybody else is delighted too, and Sketch brings down the house, at which Miss Pankerton looks superior and begins to tell me about Classical Mime by children that she once organised in large hall--seats two thousand people--near Birmingham, but I remain unresponsive, and only observe in reply that Jimmie H. of the mill is a duck, isn't he?

At this Miss P.'s eyebrows disappear into her hair, and she tells me about children she has seen in Italy who are pure Murillo types--but Our Butcher's Son here mounts the platform, in comic checks, bowler and walking-stick, and all is lost in storms of applause.

Presently Robert announces an Interval, and we all turn round in our seats and scan the room and talk to the people behind us, and someone brings forward a rumour that they've taken Close on Three Pounds at the Door, and we all agree that, considering the hot weather, it's wonderful.

IMPORTED TALENT GRACES THE PROGRAMME

Shortly afterwards Robert again ascends platform, and concert is resumed. Imported talent graces last half of the programme, in the shape of tall young gentleman who is said to be a friend of the Post Office, and who sings a doubtful comic song which is greeted with shrieks of appreciation. Our Vicar's Wife and I look at one another, and she shakes her head with a resigned expression, and whispers that it can't be helped, and she hopes the *encore* won't be any worse. It *is* worse, but not very much, and achieves enormous popular success.

By eleven o'clock all is over, someone has started God Save the King much too high, and we have all loyally endeavoured to make ourselves heard on notes that we just can't reach--Miss Pankerton has boldly attempted something that is evidently meant to be seconds, but results not happy--and we walk out into the night.

Robert drives me home. I say Weren't the children sweet? and Really, it was rather fun, wasn't it? and Robert changes gear, but makes no specific reply. Turn into our own lane, and I experience customary wonder whether house has been burnt to the ground in our absence, followed by customary reflection that anyway, the children are away at school--and then get severe shock as I see the house blazing with light from top to bottom.

Robert ejaculates, and puts his foot on the accelerator, and we dash in at gate, and nearly run into enormous blue car drawn up at front door.

I rush into the hall, and at the same moment Pamela Pringle rushes out of the drawing-room, wearing evening dress and grey fur coat with enormous collar, and throws herself on my neck. Am enabled, by mysterious process quite inexplicable to myself, to see through the back of my head that Robert has recoiled on threshold and retired with car to the garage.

Pamela P. explains that she is staying the night at well-known hotel, about forty miles away, and that when she found how near I was, she simply had to look me up, and she had simply no idea that I ever went out at night. I say that I never do, and urge her into the drawing-room, and there undergo second severe shock as I perceive it to be apparently perfectly filled with strange men. Pamela does not introduce any of them, beyond saying that it was Johnnie's car they came in, and Plum drove it. Waddell is not included in the party, nor anybody else that

I ever saw in my life, and all seem to be well under thirty, except very tall man with bald head who is referred to as Alphonse Daudet, and elderly-looking one with moustache, who I think looks Retired, probably India.

I say weakly that they must have something to drink, and look at the bell--perfectly well aware that maids have gone to bed long ago--but Robert, to my great relief, materialises and performs minor miracle by producing entirely adequate quantities of whisky-and-soda, and sherry and biscuits for Pamela and myself. After this we all seem to know one another very well indeed, and Plum goes to the piano and plays waltz tunes popular in Edwardian days. (Pamela asks at intervals What that one was called? although to my certain knowledge she must remember them just as well as I do myself.)

Towards one o'clock Pamela, who has been getting more and more affectionate towards everybody in the room, suddenly asks where the darling children are sleeping, as she would love a peep at them. Forbear to answer that if they had been at home at all, they couldn't possibly have been sleeping through conversational and musical orgy of Pamela and friends, and merely reply that both are at school. What, shrieks Pamela, that tiny weeny little dot of a Vicky at school? Am I utterly unnatural? I say Yes, I am, as quickest means of closing futile discussion, and everybody accepts it without demur, and we talk instead about Auteuil, Helen de Liman de la Pelouse--(about whom I could say a great deal more than I do)–and Pamela's imminent return home to country house where Waddell and three children await her.

Prospect of this seems to fill her with gloom, and she tells me, aside, that 'Waddell doesn't quite realise her present whereabouts, but supposes her to be crossing from Ireland to-night, and I must remember this, if he says anything about it next time we meet.

Just as it seems probable that *séance* is to continue for the rest of the night, Alphonse Daudet rises without any warning at all, says to Robert that, for his part, he's not much good at late nights, and walks out of the room. We all drift after him, Pamela announces that she is going to drive, and everybody simultaneously exclaims No, No, and Robert says that there is a leak in the radiator, and fetches water from the bathroom.

(Should have preferred him to bring it in comparatively new green enamel jug, instead of incredibly ancient and battered brass can.)

Pamela throws herself into my arms, and murmurs something of which I hear nothing at all except Remember!–like Bishop Juxon and then gets into the car, and is obliterated by Plum on one side and elderly Indian on the other.

Just as they start, Helen Wills dashes out of adjacent bushes, and is nearly run over, but this tragedy averted, and car departs.

Echoes reach us for quite twenty minutes, of lively conversation, outbreaks of song and peals of laughter, as car flies down the lane and out of sight. Robert says that they've turned the wrong way, but does not seem to be in the least distressed about it, and predicts coldly that they will all end up in local police station.

I go upstairs, all desire for sleep having completely left me, and find several drawers in dressing-table wide open, powder all over the place like snow on Mont Blanc, unknown little pad of rouge on pillow, and face-towel handsomely streaked with lip-stick.

Bathroom is likewise in great disorder, and when Robert eventually appears he brings with him small, silver-mounted comb which he alleges that he found, quite incomprehensibly, on lowest step of remote flight of stairs leading to attics. I say satirically that I hope they all felt quite at home, Robert snorts in reply, and conversation closes.

July 13th.–Life resumes its ordinary course, and next excitement will doubtless be return of Robin and Vicky from school. Am already deeply immersed in preparations for this, and Cook says that extra help will be required. I reply that I think we shall be away at the sea for at least a month--(which is not perfectly true, as much depends on financial state)–and she listens to me in silence, and repeats that help will be wanted anyway, as children make such a difference. As usual, Cook gets the last word, and I prepare to enter upon familiar and exhausting campaign in search of Extra Help.

This takes up terrific amount of time and energy, and find it wisest to resign all pretensions to literature at the moment, and adopt role of pure domesticity. Interesting psychological reaction to this--(must remember to bring it forward in discussion with dear Rose, always so intelligent)–is that I tell Robert that next year I should like to Go to America. Robert makes little or no reply, except for rather eloquent look, but nevertheless I continue to think of going to America, and taking diary with me.

THE END

Printed in Great Britain
by Amazon

45134466R00059